Books by Shirleen Davies

Historical Western Romance Series

MacLarens of Fire Mountain

Tougher than the Rest, Book One
Faster than the Rest, Book Two
Harder than the Rest, Book Three
Stronger than the Rest, Book Four
Deadlier than the Rest, Book Five
Wilder than the Rest, Book Six

Redemption Mountain

Redemption's Edge, Book One
Wildfire Creek, Book Two
Sunrise Ridge, Book Three
Dixie Moon, Book Four
Survivor Pass, Book Five

MacLarens of Boundary Mountain

Colin's Quest, Book One,
Brodie's Gamble, Book Two, Releasing 2016

<u>***Contemporary Romance Series***</u>

MacLarens of Fire Mountain

Second Summer, Book One
Hard Landing, Book Two
One More Day, Book Three
All Your Nights, Book Four
Always Love You, Book Five
Hearts Don't Lie, Book Six
No Getting Over You, Book Seven
'Til the Sun Comes Up, Book Eight, Releasing 2016

Peregrine Bay

Reclaiming Love, Book One, A Novella
Our Kind of Love, Book Two

The best way to stay in touch is to subscribe to my newsletter. Go to

www.shirleendavies.com and subscribe in the box at the top of the right column that asks for your email. You'll be notified of new books before they are released, have chances to win great prizes, and receive other subscriber-only specials.

Reclaiming Love

Peregrine Bay
Contemporary Romance Series

A Novella

SHIRLEEN DAVIES

Book One in the Peregrine Bay

Contemporary Romance Series

Avalanche Ranch Press, LLC
PO Box 12618
Prescott, AZ 86304

Book design and conversions by Joseph Murray at http://www.3rdplanetpublishing.com

Cover design by The Killion Group

ISBN: 978-1-941786-16-1

I care about quality, so if you find something in error, please contact me via email at shirleen@shirleendavies.com.

Description

Reclaiming Love – Book One, A Novella Peregrine Bay Contemporary Romance Series

Adam Monroe has seen his share of setbacks. Now he's back in Peregrine Bay, looking for a new life and second chance.

Julia Kerrigan's life rebounded after the sudden betrayal of the one man she ever loved. As president of a success real estate company, she's built a new life and future, pushing the painful past behind her.

Adam's reason for accepting the job as the town's new Police Chief can be explained in one word—Julia. He wants her back and will do whatever is necessary to achieve his goal, even knowing his biggest hurdle is the woman he still loves.

As they begin to reconnect, a terrible scandal breaks loose with Julia and Adam at the center.

Will the threat to their lives and reputations destroy their fledgling romance? Can Adam identify and eliminate the danger to Julia before he's had a chance to reclaim her love?

Dedication

This book is dedicated to all of my fans who requested a series featuring sisters as the heroines. Your input did not fall on deaf ears. Thanks so much!

Acknowledgements

Thanks also to my editor, Deborah Gunn, proofreader, Kelly Heckert, and all of my beta readers. Their insights and suggestions are greatly appreciated.

As always, many thanks to my wonderful resources, including Diane Lebow, who has been a whiz at guiding my social media endeavors, my cover designer, Kim Killion, and Joseph Murray who is a whiz at formatting my books for both print and electronic versions.

Reclaiming Love

Prologue

Peregrine Bay, Idaho, Christmas Eve

"Welcome home, Adam. I know someone who's quite anxious to see you." Joshua Kerrigan, family patriarch, stepped aside to let his oldest daughter's boyfriend walk into the large family room. Adam, a sophomore at Washington State University, had driven home the night before for the Christmas holiday. "What can I get you to drink?"

"Uh...a soda would be great. Thanks." Adam Monroe shoved his hands in his pockets and glanced around. Kerrigans always went all out decorating their house for Christmas with a tree in every room highlighting a different theme. The family room tree stood over ten feet tall, and as far back as Adam could remember, held personal ornaments and treasures of the family.

"Adam!" Julia Kerrigan ran up to him and threw her arms around his neck. "I've missed you," she murmured as her father handed Adam his drink.

"Thank you, sir." He took the glass before returning Julia's hug.

"I'll let you two catch up while I help Joannie in the kitchen."

Julia had taken special care tonight to look

good. Her deep mahogany brown hair fell in waves down her back. The long-sleeved, emerald green top clung to her slender figure and matched green eyes flecked with gold.

She grabbed Adam's hand and pulled him toward her father's study, closed the door behind them, then launched herself into his arms. It took a moment before she realized Adam continued to stand rigid, not wrapping his arms around her as he usually did and kissing her until they were both out of breath. She loosened her hold, looking up at him, noticing he refused to meet her gaze.

"Is everything all right?" Julia's heart stilled as his eyes finally met hers, a sadness she'd never seen glistened in them.

He turned away from her and walked toward a nearby wall covered floor to ceiling with the books Joshua had collected over the years. He set his drink down and once again shoved his hands into his pockets, taking a deep breath before turning toward Julia.

They'd known each other since elementary school, teased and harassed the other as they grew older, until their sophomore year in high school when they agreed not to date other people. He'd held out a solid gold St. Christopher necklace, telling her he knew it was old fashioned, but it had been the one his father had given his mother while they were in high school. His heart flipped as her eyes grew wide before a broad smile broke across her face and she fastened it around her neck.

They'd become inseparable—best friends and eventually young lovers during their senior year. Everyone assumed they'd marry after both graduated from college in a little over two years. He knew his announcement would crush her, but he'd given it a lot of thought and made up his mind.

"We need to talk."

"All right." She didn't like the sound of it as she lowered herself onto the sofa.

"I've been giving this a lot of thought, and I think we should date other people."

"Date…" her voice trailed off as the impact of his words settled in.

He walked toward her, taking a seat on a nearby chair and leaning forward. "We're nineteen. Neither of us has ever dated anyone else and now is our chance to make sure we're right for each other." Adam watched as she twisted her hands in her lap, refusing to meet his eyes. "Marriage is a big—"

"You've already met someone," she whispered as her head slowly lifted.

"It's not that—"

"But you have, haven't you?" She stood, pacing a few feet away, knowing he'd never be able to lie to her.

"Yes, I've met someone." It was all he could get out before his throat closed tight. She didn't respond, just stood frozen a few feet away. "She's a sophomore from Seattle. I..." his voice trailed off when he saw tears glisten in her eyes, her lower lip trembling as she clasped her hands in front of her. "We met last year."

She stared at him, unable to speak. Her mind raced, telling her it was a joke—one of the pranks he used to play to get her attention. Except, in her heart, she realized she'd already lost him. Julia took a step back as he walked up to her, holding out his hands, palms up.

"I don't know much about her, but..." He ran a hand through his hair. "I just feel I have to give it a shot. You and I...we're so young." He could see her inch away, trying to distance herself from both him and his declaration. "Please understand. I've given this a lot of thought, and I..." he didn't finish as she shook her head, tears streaming down her face and ran from the room. He closed his eyes, feeling more pain than he ever imagined at hurting someone he cared so much about. His legs refused to move even though he knew he should go find her, make her understand the logic of dating other people.

The door burst open before he could take a step, Julia walking in and holding out her hand.

"I won't be needing this anymore." Her voice broke but she managed to wipe away the tears, staring at him in an unwavering glare.

He opened his palm, his chest tightening as she

dropped the St. Christopher into it. He stared at it, his heart pulsing in pain.

"Julia, please, let me explain—"

She shook her head, never taking her eyes from his.

"Goodbye, Adam. I hope you've made the right decision." Before he could respond, she turned and left him to stand alone with a lifetime of memories of the two of them racing through his mind, already knowing he may have made the biggest mistake of his life.

Chapter One

Peregrine Bay, Nine years later...

"Julia, Mayor Timmons is on the phone for you."

"Thanks, Tricia. Tell him I'll be right there." Julia pushed her office door open and dropped her purse on the desk. As president of Kerrigan Real Estate and Property Management, her days started early and often lasted until late at night. As president of the local Chamber of Commerce, she also made time for interruptions by various city officials and business owners. "Good morning, Mayor, how are you?"

"Fine, fine, Julia. Look, I have a meeting in five minutes, but wanted you to know we've finally hired a new police chief."

"That's wonderful news. It took what, six months?" She rolled her eyes at the long process the council had established for the search.

"Well, you know how politics work. Anyway, I've sent the new man down to see you. If I'm not mistaken, he should be walking into your office within the next ten minutes."

"Do you have a name—"

"Hold on a minute, Julia."

She could hear the sound of muffled voices on the other end of the line.

"Sorry, Julia, but I have to run. Take care of the new chief for me."

"Of course, Mayor, but—"

She shook her head and smiled when the line went dead. She'd known the mayor her entire life. He was a distant uncle, by marriage, with a heart of gold. If he made a promise or gave his word, you could feel certain he'd make good on it. The entire town trusted him to do right by them.

"Coffee?"

Julia looked up to see her sister, Selena, walk in with an extra cup fixed the way she liked it.

"You're an angel," Julia said as she enjoyed the aroma before taking a sip. "Oh, that's good."

"So, what'd the mayor want?" Selena took a seat and crossed her legs, taking a break from her morning which had started at seven.

"They hired a new police chief. He wants us to take care of him—whatever that means."

"Is he looking to rent, buy, or build?"

"Don't know. The mayor hung up before I could ask." She took another swallow of coffee before glancing at her calendar. "Regardless, I'm passing him off to you. I'm booked today and tomorrow."

"No problem. Let me know when he gets here. What's his name?" Selena asked as Julia's intercom buzzed.

"The new police chief is here to see you. Shall I send him back?" Tricia asked.

"No, I'll be right out." Julia looked at her sister. "The mayor didn't give me his name. I'll talk to him a few minutes then find a gracious way to hand him over."

She took one more sip of coffee, checked herself in the mirror, then walked down the hall, hearing the sound of laughter coming from the lobby. She stopped to see a tall man with broad shoulders and short blonde hair joking with Tricia.

"Hello, you must be..." Her words trailed off as the man turned around, his smile fading.

"Hello, Julia."

She froze, and for an instant, she would've sworn her heart stopped beating. She took a step forward, praying her eyes deceived her, knowing they hadn't.

"Adam. It's been a long time."

"Nine years, I believe." He took a step toward her, letting his gaze wander over the woman he'd loved and walked away from. "You look as beautiful as I remember."

Julia told herself to breathe, reminding herself how he'd broken her heart all those years ago. She'd refused any contact with him since.

Ignoring the compliment, she looked past him to Tricia. "Hold my calls for a few minutes."

Tricia nodded, her eyes darting between the two

as they left the lobby.

"This is my office." She took a seat behind her desk, motioning to the guest chairs. "How can we help you?"

His eyes narrowed on hers, realizing there'd be no forgiveness from Julia. Every bond between them had been destroyed in minutes—the same minutes he wished he could wipe from their history.

He cleared his throat and pulled a sheet of paper from a pocket. "I start work in two weeks and need a place to live. I'm moving from Spokane."

"Do you have a house to sell?" She picked up her pen and began to take notes, finding strength in doing what she knew so well.

"Uh, no. Just an apartment."

"So, you'll be renting?"

"No, not unless I have no other choice. I should have enough for a down payment. Three bedrooms, two baths, not too far from town, but with some privacy." He looked up. "And a yard."

She set her pen down, feeling the walls close in on her as he spoke. He'd left messages for her within weeks of their breakup, even showing up at her parents' home the following spring break. Her father had been polite, but shut him down cold. It didn't dissuade him from trying several more times before accepting she wouldn't allow him any opening for a second chance.

"Have you put in the paperwork to prequalify

for a loan?"

"No. I didn't know I needed to."

Julia stood, unable to stay in such close proximity to him any longer. "I think we have enough to get started. You'll be working with the head of our real estate sales group. She can help you apply for a loan."

"I hoped to work with you."

"I don't do sales any longer and don't know the market as well as the others," she lied. "She'll do a much better job for you than I can. If you have a minute, I'd like to introduce you."

She poked her head into the office next door. "I'd like you to meet our new police chief."

Adam stood behind Julia, looking over her shoulder to the young woman seated at the desk.

"Selena?"

"My God. Adam Monroe. You're the new police chief?" She walked toward him, holding out her hand. "Congratulations." She glanced at Julia, and seeing the distress in her eyes, understood the situation without it being explained. "I'm guessing you'll need a place to live."

"Yes, I will."

"I've taken notes." Julia handed a sheet of paper to Selena, then turned toward Adam. "Let me welcome you back to Peregrine Bay. I hope you've made the right decision."

His gaze followed her down the hall, her parting

words hit him like a punch to his gut—the same words she'd spoken to him the night he'd broken up with her. He slowly turned back to see Selena studying him. She lowered her eyes to read the information Julia provided and decide how best to handle the unexpected appearance of the man who'd caused Julia so much pain.

"I guess it would be best to give you some information on neighborhoods and review the open listings. We can then schedule visits to the ones you'd like to see."

He glanced over his shoulder before taking a seat, wishing he'd had a few more minutes with Julia. "All right."

******

Julia slumped into her chair, her heart pounding. It had taken years to get past the fact her best friend, the one man she'd ever loved, had walked away. He'd attended Washington State on a baseball scholarship while she'd gone south to Boise State. Friends of hers who went to WSU had let her know his new interest was a cheerleader—a bouncy, bubbly brunette who'd hounded him mercilessly during baseball season his freshman year.

Tall, handsome, and a star athlete, Julia had always understood her good fortune at being the one he wanted. She'd put everything into their relationship, driving to Pullman to see his games, responding to every request he made of her to attend events and dances. Not once had she suspected someone else had their eyes set on him, or that he returned the interest.

Even now, nine years later, her chest tightened in pain.

She noticed the time, realizing she had a meeting with her CPA in ten minutes. Grabbing her purse, she dashed from the office, rushing to her car. Selena would take care of Adam, find him a home far away from where Julia lived. She'd seldom seen the previous police chief and saw no reason it would be different with the new one.

She'd push him from her mind, steel her heart, and continue on as she had since the Christmas Eve she'd never been able to forget.

******

"Let me make some calls. Is nine o'clock tomorrow too early to start?" Selena asked as they stood in the lobby.

"No, that's fine." Adam looked around, hoping for one more look at Julia before leaving. He held out a piece of paper. "Here's my phone number and where I'm staying."

"Plan on meeting me here. We'll take my car." She saw his brows draw together as his mouth curved up at the ends. "Don't worry. I'm a much better driver than I was when you and Julia were together." She noticed him wince and wished she'd kept her mouth shut. "Anyway, it's roomy so you can stretch out."

"All right. Thanks, Selena." He held out his hand.

"My pleasure. And again, welcome back, Adam. I truly hope this turns out to be a good opportunity for you."

Adam needed to call his folks, let them know he'd taken the position. They'd moved from Peregrine Bay during his junior year in college, his dad buying a business north in Pine Cove, but still on the shores of Lake Bountiful.

Peregrine Bay lay on the south end, a beautiful spot filled with longtime residents, wealthy second home owners, and thousands of tourists during the summer months. He hoped to find a home at the north end of the bay, making his drive to visit his parents about an hour.

"Hi, Mom. Tell Dad I accepted the job. Yes, I feel good about the decision. I'll tell you all about it at supper." He pocketed the phone and pulled into traffic, turning toward the lake, knowing he was searching for the sense of belonging he'd lost. He swallowed the lump in his throat. Perhaps, if all went well, he'd be able to find what he'd carelessly walked away from all those years ago.

Chapter Two

"Here's the next one. We'll stop for lunch after this and review the homes we'll visit this afternoon." Selena pulled to a stop and grabbed the property data sheet.

"Do you think I can qualify for this one?" Adam asked, doubting he had the money for what he saw. The house looked large from the outside. It sat on a large lot on the shore of the lake, about a mile from the north end of town.

She smiled. "Trust me. Once you see the inside, you'll know why this one is in your price range." She unlocked the door, letting him step inside ahead of her.

"Holy..." Adam began, then clamped his mouth shut. A musty odor slammed into him as he took in the filth. Cigarette butts littered the old, shag carpet, sockets fell from outlets, and the walls sported an odd yellowish-brown color as if they hadn't been cleaned or painted in years. He cleared his throat. "What color do you think this was?" He nodded toward the walls.

"I know they were white as I sold this house to the current owner five years ago. From what I understand, several men rented this place for four years, never lifting a hand to clean. Nothing was ever reported to the landlord, so little has been repaired. They up and moved out on him a few months ago. The owner is in a convalescent home. His relatives live in Chicago and have little to do with him. At this point he just wants to get rid of it." She wiggled her eyebrows at him.

Adam followed her toward a large room divided into a kitchen, eating area, and family room with sliding glass doors to a huge deck. The view to the lake alone had to be worth tens of thousands of dollars.

"You'd need to do a lot of work, but the electrician and plumber I had over last week said the repairs in those areas are pretty minor. You'd need to replace a few fixtures, change some lights, repaint, add new flooring, and buy appliances. If you look to your left, there's a mudroom between the kitchen and garage."

Adam pushed the door open, seeing an old washer and dryer. His breath caught when he stepped down into the garage.

"This must hold four cars."

"Yep. The person who built it had two cars, a truck, and a boat. All fit inside, plus there's a carport on the other side of the garage. As I recall, the original owner used it for his boat trailer."

By the time they'd completed the tour, Adam's initial shock had worn off. Four bedrooms, three baths, three fireplaces, a family room plus a den off the master. It sat on a full acre and included a boat dock.

"What do you think?" Selena asked, seeing the look of concentration on Adam's face.

He walked around the back yard once more. It would be a lot of work, but he could do almost all of it himself, although he'd have to rent a place for a few months.

"It's everything on the list, plus more. How much?" he asked, holding his breath.

Selena named a price, feeling a sense of satisfaction at the relief on Adam's face.

"You're kidding?"

"Nope. I sold it to the current owner. He called me last week and gave me the listing. The man just wants out."

"The roof?" Adam asked.

"He put a new one on when he bought it five years ago. It still has ten years on the warranty. Plus, he added the deck and boat dock."

"You know the rest of the properties on the list today. What do you think?" He couldn't take his eyes off the lake. His dad would have a great time fishing here, and his mom would love the kitchen once he fixed it up.

"Buy it, Adam. You may never get a second chance at something like this."

He rubbed the back of his neck with his hand. It

seemed he didn't get many second chances since his sophomore year in college. He wouldn't miss this opportunity.

"Let's do it."

******

Selena handed the offer to Adam then sat back to finish her lunch. "With the down payment you're offering and the fact I know you, I don't believe the seller will have a problem accepting."

Adam read and signed the document. "I hope you're right. I can't go any higher on the price since I'll need money to fix it up."

"He knows it needs work and is prepared for something in this range." She drank her soda, fidgeting with the straw while she watched him. "Tell me what you've been up to. We all thought you'd go pro after college."

His face clouded before he steeled his expression. "I tore some stuff up in my arm and it never healed right. Can't pitch in the majors if you don't have an arm left."

"I'm sorry to hear it. I had a great time watching you when Julia would let me tag along to Pullman. You were real good."

"Yeah, well, what's good is that I decided to get a degree in criminal justice, so I had a fall back plan in place. Spokane police hired me right out of school. I got my master's degree and moved up to detective. I'd just applied for the U.S. Marshal Service when I got the call from the mayor. It seemed right, plus it would be close to my folks." He shrugged, knowing the real reason he accepted the job was Julia. Friends had told him she never married and didn't seem to have anyone serious in her life. Adam didn't count Mark Walters, a boy they grew up with who he heard she'd been seeing on a casual basis the last few months. Perhaps, if he played it right...

"Uh, oh."

He glanced up at Selena's comment to see Julia talking to the restaurant hostess before following her across the room. A moment later, Mark walked in and found her table.

"Is she dating Mark?" He turned toward Selena, noting she'd also seen Julia and Mark arrive.

"It's not really my place to say, but yes. Sort of."

"Sort of?" Adam turned his attention to Selena, raising an eyebrow.

She folded her napkin and set it on the table, deciding how to answer.

"He treats her well, is solid, dependable—"

"Boring."

Selena let out a small chuckle. "Well, yes. He's comfortable." She threw him a pointed glare. "And, she trusts him."

"Ouch. I guess I deserved that."

"I like you, Adam. You were the absolute best thing to ever happen to Julia—and the worst. People in town talked about the split, saying you'd found someone fun and, well...free spirited, to replace her."

"What the hell?" Adam never heard any of the gossip regarding the breakup.

"I was thankful she lived in Boise and didn't have to hear it in person. She stayed down there to get her master's degree. By the time she returned to Peregrine Bay, the commotion had died down. Of course, it helped that you jettisoned the cheerleader within months."

Adam grimaced. He'd been stupid, rash, and immature, walking away from Julia and everything they'd built. Having your best friend as your lover didn't seem uncommon until he'd lost her. It didn't take long to realize most people never found someone as devoted, loving, or trusting, and he'd thrown it all away.

"If you're thinking of a second try, realize she's not the same person you knew. Please don't make a move unless you're prepared to stick it out." She finished her soda. "And even then, the odds aren't close to being in your favor."

******

"Julia, you with me?" Mark asked, realizing her thoughts were miles away.

"I'm sorry. I have this proposal to prepare and it's been on my mind." The proposal had crossed her mind. Adam Monroe and his return as police chief consumed her thoughts, although she'd never admit it to anyone.

He jiggled his phone in front of her and gave an impatient nod. "We have supper at my parents' house on Friday night at seven and the cocktail party on Sunday at the club."

She checked her calendar, shaking her head. "I don't have either in my schedule, Mark. Are you certain you told me?"

"Of course I am. Both are important. Everyone who matters in Peregrine Bay will be at the cocktail party."

She rolled her eyes at his smug remark. "Not everyone. I have a reception for the chamber on Sunday afternoon to introduce the new police chief. As the president, I'll be attending it and not the Bay Club cocktail event."

"And Friday?" The tone of his voice revealed his displeasure at her decision to attend the chamber event instead of the summer social kickoff.

"I'll do my best. I have a five o'clock meeting with the developer of the large parcel on the southeast shore. He's in town for one night before he flies to Seattle."

"Surely the meeting won't last more than two hours," he sniffed.

"The last one took five hours. I've already made plans to have dinner delivered." She glanced once more at her calendar then looked up to see Selena and Adam leave. She hadn't seen them when she arrived. To her relief, neither looked in her direction as they made their way outside. As much as she didn't want Adam back in their hometown, she'd also learned of his qualifications from the mayor and council members. He'd packed a lot of experience into his time with the Spokane PD. She had to admit, it appeared he'd make an exceptional police chief.

"Are you finished?" Mark asked, picking up the check, then straightening his suit jacket.

"I am sorry about not being able to make dinner with your parents. Please give them my best."

"You know, Julia, at some point a choice will need to be made."

She tilted her head to one side, narrowing her eyes. "Choice?"

"I don't see much of a future for us if you aren't willing to make a few sacrifices."

"You knew my work commitment when we began to see each other. Besides we agreed to keep our relationship casual. Nothing has changed. I believe we've both made sacrifices in deference to our jobs, and I'm sorry if you feel otherwise." Julia slung her purse over her shoulder, heading for the door, ignoring Mark's disgruntled sigh.

"Look, we obviously won't see each other this weekend. I'll call you Monday. We can have lunch, dinner, whatever you want." Mark slid a hand into one pocket, jiggling his car keys—a nervous habit which drove Julia crazy.

"Fine. Have a pleasant weekend." She gave him a slight peck on the cheek, then turned toward her office, wondering why she kept seeing him. The answer was obvious. Most of the time, dating Mark was comfortable and convenient. His manners were impeccable even if his disposition sometimes soured over the least little slight, and she never had to worry about having an escort to a major event.

She let out a groan at the thought of sleeping with him. He'd made it clear that's what he wanted, but she'd always declined. She'd never felt the least amount of spark and refused to sleep with him out of a sense of obligation.

Julia let her thoughts drift back to one of the times she and Adam made love. He'd driven to Boise as a surprise, taken her out to dinner and a movie. Then he'd escorted her into one of the nicest hotels in the city and calmly walked into the elevator, pushing the button for the twelfth floor. She'd always remember it—room 1212.

He pushed the door open, and waited to see the expression on her face. Twelve bouquets adorned the room, one for each year since they'd begun paying attention to each other in the fifth grade. He grabbed her hand, slowly walked to the bed, and turned her to him, claiming her mouth with his. The result had been the most passionate and memorable night of her life.

"Good afternoon, Julia."

She snapped back to the present, realizing she'd lost track of time and location. She'd walked a full block past her office.

"Oh, good afternoon, Mr. Jost. Beautiful day, don't you think?"

He stood outside his jewelry store, the nicest in town, and the most expensive. Adam had purchased a beautiful ring with her birthstone from him at five dollars a week until he'd paid it off. Her heart squeezed at the memory before she brushed the sentiment aside and straightened her back.

"Indeed it is a beautiful day. I hear young Adam Monroe is our new police chief. It's hard to believe he's old enough to hold such an important position." He scratched his chin before his eyes widened. "Say, didn't the two of you date for a while?"

She swallowed and nodded. "Yes, for a while. Well, I'd better get back to the office."

"Hey, Julia."

She glanced across the street to see one of her other sisters, Calypso, dash across to join her. Calypso led the property management group at the company and was her half-sister, as were the two youngest twin girls, Danielle and Lily. Her father had been married three times with she and Selena having the same mother, Calypso another, and the twins another—their father's current, and longest lasting wife, Joannie. The oldest three were involved in the business while the twins attended college in Boise.

"What's up with you today? I saw you walking like you were in some kind of fog, missing the office and almost getting blindsided crossing the street," Caly joked.

"I did not," Julia laughed. "I haven't seen you all week. Where've you been hiding yourself?"

"Meeting with our new landscape firm at all the properties, getting repairs done at the Main Street apartments, installing a new kitchen in unit A at the Mountain View duplex—"

"Okay, I get it. You've been busy."

"Not too busy to know who's been hired as the new police chief. Have you seen him?" Caly had been real fond of Adam, teasing him, and generally being a pest whenever he came to see Julia. She'd been five years younger than her oldest sister, and at fifteen, too wrapped up in her own world to understand the pain her sister felt when Adam left. Even now, she somehow couldn't understand why Julia couldn't let bygones be bygones and move on.

"Uh...yes, I've seen Adam. Selena is helping him find a house. Look, I'd better get inside." Before she could turn, Caly put a hand on her arm to stop her.

"I know I can be an idiot sometimes, but I do remember how much he meant to you. If you want, I'll find some guys to rough him up, see if he's worthy of being our police chief."

Julia couldn't help laughing at the picture Caly painted. At over six feet tall, broad, and well-built, it would take a few men to drag Adam down. She wrapped an arm around her sister. "Thanks. I needed the laugh."

Chapter Three

"Thanks. I'll have the paperwork to you within the hour." She hung up and smiled. "He accepted your offer, pending loan approval. He wants to close in thirty days instead of forty-five, if it's all right with you."

Adam blew out a breath. "That's great. Wonderful, in fact."

"You'll want an inspection. Do you have someone in mind?"

"No one."

"Then I'll arrange it for you as well as the appraisal. It will take two to three weeks to get it all done. How about meeting me at the house for the inspection? You can take notes of what you want to do, measure, and start ordering supplies. It will give you a jump-start on the project. I'll set it up for next week, before you start your new job."

"Yeah, about that. Mayor Timmons called and wants me to start this Monday instead. I'm certain I can make time to make the appointment. Just let me know when."

"Sounds good. Oh, and I guess I'll see you at the reception on Sunday."

Adam's brows knit together as he tilted his

head. "What reception?"

"Didn't Mayor Timmons tell you about the reception to introduce you to the town?"

He groaned at the news. "No. Guess he forgot."

"Here." She handed him the invitation which had been delivered the day before. "Yours may be waiting for you at your address in Spokane," she joked. "Government efficiency and all that."

"It says it's at the Lake Bountiful restaurant—never heard of it."

"That's because father just opened it a year ago at the Landing. It's his new center on the lake. Follow Lake Drive around the lake to the east until you see the old bait shop. It's right past the new light signal."

"Lots of changes since I left." He made a mental note to drive around the area Friday and Saturday to get a better feel for all the changes. "I'll see you Sunday."

The bright afternoon sun hit him in the face as he stepped outside, almost running into two women.

"Adam Monroe. That is you, right?" Calypso asked as Adam moved aside.

"Yes." He stared at the woman standing next to Julia, trying to place her.

"Don't tell me you don't recognize me?"

His eyes narrowed on her before everything clicked. "Caly?"

"That's right. It's good to see you. And congratulations on the new job."

He glanced at Julia, seeing her move away as if trying to create some space between them. "Thanks. I just got this from Selena." He held out the invitation. "Appears Mayor Timmons forgot to let me know."

Caly laughed. "Sounds like him. I'll be there and of course Julia will be." She looked toward her sister. "You know she's the president of the chamber this year."

"No. I guess I didn't get that memo either." Adam slid the invitation into his pocket and checked his watch. "I'd better get going. I'm supposed to pick up my uniform, gear, and sign some more paperwork. Timmons asked me to start a week early so I'm scrambling. I'll see both of you Sunday." He touched a finger to the brim of his hat then turned toward his truck.

Caly waited until he was a good distance away before letting out a breath accompanied by a low whistle. "Wow."

"Yeah. It's a real bitch." Julia continued to stare as he climbed into the truck.

"You mean about him becoming a real hunk?"

"Too bad he hasn't turned to flab with a pot belly. Not that I care one way or the other," she sighed. "Let me know if there's anything I can do to help with the work at the apartments. I plan to take off by six this evening, but can stick around if you need me."

"Nope. I have it all covered." Caly pursed her lips then put a hand on Julia's arm. "How about I stop by tonight, bring food, and we get snockered on wine?"

It had been a while since she'd spent an evening with her younger sister. "Sounds great. Chinese?"

"Works for me. I'll let Selena know. See you about seven." Caly took off down the hall, disappearing into her office.

Julia took one more look toward the street, trying not to wonder what Adam did with his evenings now that he was back in town. It wouldn't be long before all the eligible women were throwing themselves at him. He'd have his pick. She shifted her attention back to work, reminding herself what he did with his time didn't concern her.

"Julia. Jamison Denning is holding on line two," Tricia said, breaking her from her mental ramblings. "He needs to reschedule your meeting on Friday."

Julia groaned. That would leave her free to go with Mark to his parents' house. Well, she just wouldn't tell him about the change. A Friday night alone sounded pretty good right now.

"Fine. Fit him in whenever he's available." She glanced at her watch. Four o'clock and nothing on her desk which couldn't wait until tomorrow. "I'm heading home early, Tricia. Unless something urgent comes up, I'll see you in the morning." She didn't even check her office before leaving.

She slipped into her almost new sports car she'd agonized over purchasing a few weeks before, glad both Selena and Calypso had pushed her to buy it. Every time she sat at the wheel a smile broke out across her face. She'd just turned the key when she heard a tap on her window and saw Tricia standing next to the car.

"I almost forgot. These came for you." She handed Julia a bouquet of roses. "Here's the note. Sorry, I didn't have time to put them in water."

"No problem. I'll see you tomorrow."

Julia set the bouquet and note on the passenger seat, certain Mark had sent them to her. She drove toward home, passing a new women's boutique she'd been wanting to check out and pulled into a parking place. She really did need something new for the reception on Sunday. Forgetting all about the flowers and note, she walked inside, introduced herself to the new owner and started poking through the dresses, pulling out a few before disappearing into a dressing room.

An hour later she dropped her purchases into the trunk, pleased with what she'd found. She still had an hour before Calypso arrived. She set the bouquet and note on the kitchen counter before changing into something comfortable, and pouring a glass of wine. Might as well get a head start, she thought, putting on a CD and collapsing into her favorite chair.

A loud pounding shocked her upright. She pushed out of the chair, still dazed from her unplanned nap.

"You started without us?" Caly asked when she spotted the glass of wine.

"Not really, although I gave it a try. I must have dozed off as soon as I hit the chair." She rubbed her eyes with the palms of her hands. "Come on. We'll get plates."

"Who sent flowers?" Selena asked, picking up the bouquet.

"Must've been Mark. I didn't check." Her voice sounded raspy from sleep.

"I'll put them in water—" Selena started.

"And I'll read the note," Caly said. "Hmmm, no name. It just says, *To a beautiful lady*." She handed it to Julia.

"Well, it has to be from him. No one else would send flowers." She set it aside and grabbed two more wine glasses, noticing the look which passed between her sisters. "What?"

"Nothing," Selena replied, nudging Caly and picking up her glass. "Here's to the three of us," she toasted and took a small sip.

"You're not going to nurse one drink all evening are you?" Caly asked Selena.

"Hey, one glass is a lot for me, remember? I'm not the party girl you are."

"Neither is Julia, but she manages to get down two or three glasses during girl's night."

Julia ignored both as she poked through the carryout boxes of Chinese. "Sesame chicken, broccoli beef, fried rice, and...uh, mystery vegetables." She scrunched up her face and lifted her gaze to Caly.

"Buddha's Delight."

"Ah."

They filled their plates and dug in, enjoying the food before Caly broke the silence.

"What are you going to do about him?" she asked Julia.

Julia gave her a blank stare. "Who?"

"Adam, of course. I mean, we all know Mark isn't for you—not long term anyway. You ought to cut the poor man loose."

"Which, by the way, is none of your business." Julia watched Caly over the rim of her glass before picking up her fork.

"Of course it is. Do you think the family wants to be stuck with someone with the personality of a turnip? Don't get me wrong, he's a nice guy. But really, what do you see in him?"

Caly's direct manner had always been her strength and greatest weakness. However, she'd never let her thoughts out about Mark until tonight.

Julia's unwavering gaze shot to Selena. "Do you feel the same?"

Selena shifted in her seat. She'd never been as frank as Caly, keeping most opinions to herself. This time she cleared her throat and squared her gaze on Julia. "Well...yes, I do."

Julia set down her fork and sat back, rolling the stem of her wine glass between her fingers before glancing up at the two of them.

"He can be pretty dull," she snickered before breaking into a laugh.

"There are dead people out there with more personality," Caly joked between her laughter.

"He's not that bad." Julia's mild protest accompanied more giggles.

"Yes, he is." Selena picked up her glass and took another sip, smiling.

"But he's—"

"Safe. Yes we know. You might as well admit to the world you've decided to stop living if you keep seeing him."

"Isn't that a little harsh?" Julia asked, filling her glass once more.

"Nope," Caly answered. "It's accurate."

Julia sobered at the sincerity in Caly's voice.

"If either of you is thinking I'll dump Mark because Adam is back, forget it. First, he walked away from me. Other than a few attempts to explain, he's never given any indication he regretted his decision. Second, I don't love him anymore. Third, the man is going to have hordes of single women after him and I refuse to be part of the stampeding herd. And fourth, if I do stop seeing Mark, it will have everything to do with him being tedious, unspontaneous, and a fun sponge, not because I've found someone else." She emptied her glass and glared at them.

"Fun sponge?" Caly blurted out, holding her stomach as laughter once again consumed her.

"Well, you know...boring...monotonous..." Julia flicked her hand a couple of times in the air before standing to grab the phone on the second ring. "Hello." She heard nothing. "Hello. Is someone there?" She waited a moment than hung up. "Must've been a wrong number. Anyway, where were we?"

"You were pouring another glass of wine and describing Mark as a fun sponge," Selena responded, enjoying the banter. "By the way, someone who is definitely not a fun sponge found a house today and the owner has made a verbal acceptance."

"Already? That didn't take long." A part of Julia hoped Adam wouldn't find anything, become disillusioned with his job, give up, and leave. She did realize it was a delusional thought as he never gave up on anything—except them. "Which home?"

"It's the new listing on the lake. He loved it."

"Doesn't it require a lot of work?" Julia sat back down, crossing her arms.

"It does, but I believe that added to its appeal. Adam can make it his own. He's pretty excited about it."

"Good for him. He can turn it into a full-blown bachelor pad and have at it." This time a hint of bitterness laced her words.

"I don't get the sense he's into the party scene." Selena knew how much Julia hated hearing about Adam. As a client, and the new police chief, she thought her sister had to find a way to deal with the unpleasant memories and move past them.

"He wanted a place closer to his mom and dad in Pine Cove, but I believe owning property on the lake sealed the sale. Adam mentioned he tries to swim several times a week for exercise and to relax. I know he has plans to expand the deck for a fishing boat and the extra storage shed got his attention. I guess he has a lot of camping and hiking gear. He started rock climbing the last few years and already purchased a membership to Kelly's Gym."

"It seems the two of you caught up quite a bit in just a couple of days." Julia's sarcasm wasn't lost on her sisters as she uncorked another bottle of wine and filled her glass, quirking an eyebrow at Selena.

"Don't even go there." Selena held up her hand, indicating she'd have none of what Julia insinuated. "We both know it's my job to learn about a client so

I can recommend the best choices. Besides, I thought you might find the information useful."

"For what?" She directed an incredulous look at Selena.

Selena leaned forward in her chair, her eyes shining with purpose. "When you see him Sunday at the reception. It'll give you something to talk about."

"Thanks for the assistance, but I'm pretty certain I can handle it."

"Right," Caly said. "By running in the opposite direction. In fact, I'll bet you dinner you can't handle a conversation with him for more than ten minutes—just the two of you."

"That's ridiculous. Of course I can talk with him for ten minutes."

"The two of you with no one else around?" Selena asked.

"Absolutely.

Caly rolled her eyes.

"I saw that." Julia pointed the wine glass at her. "And, I'll take that bet."

Chapter Four

Julia hit the snooze button once more, pulled the pillow on top of her head and groaned. They'd finished two bottles of wine last night, which meant she and Calypso had done most of the drinking, leaving Selena to be Caly's designated driver—again.

Julia hadn't taken a day off in months. Today it sounded pretty good. Her appointment with the developer had been cancelled and any other work could be completed from home. She picked up her phone, sent a text message to Tricia, then padded to the bathroom to down a couple aspirins. All she needed was another hour of sleep to calm her pounding headache then she might be able to handle food in her queasy stomach. She laid back down on the bed and closed her eyes, trying to find the sleep her body craved. Instead, her mind drifted over all that had happened the last week.

She had two days before the reception for Adam when she'd have to make good on her bet with Calypso. Ever since he'd shown up at her office, she'd been plagued with images of the two of them— talking, laughing, loving—images she'd been successful at pushing to the far recesses of her mind for years. Now they flooded back to haunt her, interfering with not just her sleep, but her ability to focus at work. And, due to wine and pride, she'd committed to placing herself in front of him for at least ten minutes, alone, with no way to ignore him short of being rude.

Of course, she could simply concede, pay Calypso the bet, and be done with it. Taking her sister to dinner wasn't the worst bet to lose. Unfortunately, her sisters would interpret forfeiting the wager as an admission she still held feelings for Adam, and she wasn't ready for anyone else to know the truth of it. Julia massaged her eyes with the heels of her palms, then stared at the ceiling, acknowledging she'd get no more sleep.

She felt a good measure better by the time she showered and slipped into a pair of well-worn jeans, white cotton top, and sandals. Two cups of coffee later, she'd finished responding to emails and cleared her voice mail at work. From a drawer, she retrieved the list of errands she wanted to run if she ever had a day off, scanning it and deciding which items to tackle today.

Her first stop would be to deliver donations to the local thrift store. She grabbed her purse, lifted the box filled with clothes out of the front closet, deposited it in the trunk of her car, then backed out of the garage. She glanced at her front porch and stopped. A blue box with a white ribbon sat on one of the Adirondack chairs. It was tempting to ignore it. Instead, Julia walked up the steps, noting no message accompanied the box, already knowing it had to be from Mark. Lifting the lid, her eyes widened at what appeared to be a dozen yellow roses with a white envelope perched on top. She tore it open and read the message.

A woman can never have too many roses.

She turned it over, but like the one from the day before, there was no signature or indication of the shop who delivered it. Tucking the note in her jeans, she carried the roses inside, put them in a vase with water and took off. Her first stop would now be one of the two flower shops in town.

******

"Good morning, Chief Monroe. Can I help you?" Tricia asked. Thanks to Calypso, she now knew some of the history between Monroe and her boss, Julia. She liked to think of herself as non-judgmental, but she couldn't help but feel a bit of disapproval for the man.

"Is Julia in?" He pulled the hat from his head and fingered the brim, glancing down the hall toward her office.

"She's taking the day off, but Selena is due in any minute. Would you like to wait for her?"

"Actually, it's Julia I need to speak with. Will she be in tomorrow?"

Tricia made a show of looking at the calendar, already knowing her boss hadn't missed a Saturday since before Christmas. "She doesn't have any appointments, but I expect she'll be by at some point." She glanced up, noticing the slightest amount of turmoil cross his face, and decided to go easy on him. "Her habit is to stop for bagels and coffee around nine. Why don't you come by about nine-thirty?"

"Thanks. I'll do that."

Adam stepped out into the bright sunlight. He'd forgotten how beautiful summer mornings were in Peregrine Bay. Growing up, he'd spent as many Saturday mornings fishing as he could—at least those when he hadn't had baseball practice. Sometimes he even squeezed in a couple of hours on Sundays before church. Julia had come with him many times, becoming darn good at catching the elusive, yet beautiful, golden trout that inhabited their section of Lake Bountiful. They'd sit around, cleaning their catch and laughing, often ending up in a water fight. His chest squeezed at the memory. He shook his head, knowing all he could do now was move forward and hope he could find some way to get Julia to move forward with him.

He settled his hat on his head and started down the sidewalk, stopping to introduce himself to business owners he hadn't met. The owner of the jewelry store, Mr. Jost, swept the sidewalk outside his store, waved and motioned for Adam to come over.

"Good morning, Adam. Congratulations on the new job." Jost shook his hand, then resumed sweeping as he spoke. "It's good to have you home."

"Thanks. Is Mrs. Jost inside?" He glanced through the door, seeing no one through the glass insert.

"You've been gone a long time, Adam. My wife passed a couple of years ago."

Adam's gaze shifted back to the elderly man. He'd known them long before the day he'd walked in to buy the birthstone ring for Julia. "I'm sorry. I never heard about it."

Jost set the broom aside and looked toward the shop. "She was helping a customer when she grabbed her chest and collapsed. Never woke up." He let out a sigh, then glanced at Adam and shook his head. "Doc says she had no pain. Gone just like that." He snapped his fingers before gripping the broom handle with both hands. "Julia Kerrigan stopped by a couple days ago."

Adam pursed his lips, not certain how to respond.

"Have you seen her?" Jost asked.

"Uh...yes. I contacted them when I first accepted the job. I'm working with Selena to buy a house."

"You should've married that girl." He stopped

sweeping long enough to cast a glance at Adam, putting a hand on his hip. "Looks like you have a second chance."

Adam smiled at the man's ramblings, wishing it were as simple as Jost made it seem. "She's seeing someone."

He let out a snort. "Mark Walters? I figure that boy will last a few weeks, month tops, now that you're back."

"Maybe so. Julia and I haven't talked much."

He leaned on the broom, fixing Adam with an incredulous look. "You married?"

"No, sir."

"Engaged?"

"No, sir."

"Same with Julia and there's a reason for that." He glanced at his watch. "It's time I ate lunch. You think about what I said."

Adam watched, his mouth slightly open, a smile curving up the corners of his mouth as Mr. Jost disappeared inside. The old man had always been direct and a firm believer he and Julia were meant to be together. He'd almost thrown Adam out of his shop the summer after they'd broken up. Instead, he'd told Adam not to come back around until he got his head out of his ass.

He turned toward the street, his eyes settling on the flower shop as a familiar figure stepped inside. Adam dashed across the street and into the small store, standing to the side, watching as Julia talked with the owner.

"You're certain these aren't from here?" he heard Julia ask.

"I am. We have white, red, gold, and silver boxes. Nothing in blue. You may want to check the other shop." Her gaze lifted from the counter to see Adam. "Well, the new Police Chief."

"Good morning." He took off his hat as he walked forward.

"Congratulations on your new position."

"Thank you, ma'am." He shot a glance at Julia, noting the box of yellow roses. "Nice flowers. I'm guessing they're from Mark Walters."

"How do you know about Mark?"

He chuckled. "Not much has changed, Julia. You stand on the street corner for thirty minutes and learn everything important about the town. It's my first stop each day." He looked out the front window. "That corner bus stop over there. Perfect for catching gossip."

A laugh escaped the shop owner's lips before she looked at Julia, who narrowed her eyes at him.

"If that's your story, fine. And who they're from is none of your business." She replaced the top, scooped up the box and headed for the door.

"Julia, wait. I do have a question for you."

"What is it, Chief Monroe?" She turned toward him, trying not to look at the t-shirt which stretched across his taut chest.

"I'd rather you call me Adam."

She tilted her head, focusing on him while growing impatient as the heat in the small shop began to rise. He seemed taller and more rugged than she remembered, with what appeared to be a permanent tan which matched the caramel highlights in his eyes. Faint crow's feet appeared at the corners of each eye when he grinned, as he did now, causing a sharp pain to slice through her.

"Julia, you all right?"

"Uh...yes. Sorry."

"About Sunday's reception. I assume you want me to wear my uniform." He stared at her, standing less than a foot away, and wondered where her mind had drifted off to.

"That would be fine. Well, I'd better go." She grabbed the door handle as his hand settled on her arm.

"Do you have plans for lunch?"

She glanced down then up at his face, moistening her lips, having no idea the affect this small movement had on Adam. "No, I mean, yes. What I mean is, I have a long list of things to get done and won't have time for lunch." She turned toward the door then glanced over her shoulder. "I'll see you Sunday."

******

Julia tapped her foot on the ground as she waited for Mark's assistant to get back on the line. She'd blown through her errands, finishing in time to grab a deli sandwich and soda, before locating a vacant picnic table at the park by the water.

"Ms. Kerrigan?"

"I'm here."

"Mr. Walters said he's sorry he can't pick up the call, but he didn't send you anything. Is there some problem?"

Julia's mind went blank. She had no idea who, except Mark, would send her roses—and twice within twenty-four hours. "No, there's no problem. Thanks for checking."

She watched the sun disappear behind the western mountains, knowing there was just one other person who might have sent them. He'd done it several times during high school and college. Somehow, it didn't make sense he'd send them now, not after all these years and for no apparent reason. Well, she'd still confront Adam, making it clear she wanted nothing from him and certainly not flowers.

Julia started the engine as her phone rang. "Hello."

"It's Mark. What's going on?"

"Nothing really. Someone sent me flowers and I thought it must have been you." He didn't respond right away, although she could hear his faint breathing on the other end.

"A secret suitor, Julia?" His tone told Julia he didn't find it at all amusing. "Or, perhaps the new police chief. Are you seeing him?"

He hadn't brought up Adam before, even though he knew their history.

"Of course not. That ended years ago." She pursed her lips, not wanting to get into a discussion about Adam.

"I can't help you. I guess this is something you'll need to figure out on your own. I've a client waiting." He hung up without another word, indicating the level of irritation he felt over her inability to attend his events this weekend, and now, the flowers.

Julia dropped the phone into her purse and gripped the steering wheel. She needed to call it off with Mark, and soon.

Chapter Five

"Eighteen, nineteen, twenty. That's good, Julia. Let's move to the next machine."

Her personal trainer, Troy Layman, and his wife, Kelly, owned the popular gym in the center Julia's father owned and Calypso managed. Julia had appointments twice during the week and every Saturday.

"Have you seen Adam?" Troy asked as he set up the weights at the next machine. The four had known each other since grade school, double dating many times in high school before they left for college. The difference was, Troy and Kelly had made it—she and Adam hadn't. Their shared past had never come up, until now.

"Yes, a couple of times. Selena is helping him buy a house." She positioned herself as he indicated and began the routine.

"He bought a membership at the gym. Kelly gave him our friends and family discount." He flashed her a grin.

"Free?" she huffed as he held up a hand to stop her.

"Darn close. Okay, wait a minute and do another rep, then repeat once more. I'm going to check on a new member."

She relaxed, closing her eyes while remembering a day the summer between their junior and senior years in high school when the four of them attended the state fair. They'd eaten hot dogs, turkey legs, onion rings, milk shakes, and funnel cakes, then rode each ride at least twice. The concert had been standing room only, but no one cared. Adam had pulled into her parents' driveway at two in the morning, earning him a stern reprimand from Joshua Kerrigan, and Julia three days of being allowed no calls from him. The consequences were negligible compared to the memories and good times.

"Are you finished?" a familiar, deep voice asked.

Julia let her eyes flutter open to see Adam standing next to her in his workout clothes, a towel in his hand. For an instant she smiled, forgetting it wasn't twelve years before and they weren't in high school. She cleared her throat as the smile disappeared from her face.

"Give me a few minutes and you can have the machine."

"I can spot for—"

"No...I can handle it." She completed two more reps, grabbed her towel, and walked past him, not making eye contact. "It's yours."

"Julia, hold up."

She didn't turn, but did stop, allowing him to

catch up with her.

"Look, I know this isn't the time or place, but we've got to work something out. You run a successful business and I'm the police chief. We *are* going to be seeing each other whether you want to or not." He ran a hand through his hair, glancing around to be sure no one overheard them. "Can't we find some neutral ground?"

She took a breath and swiped the towel across her face to erase the moisture. "You're right. We need to talk. How about tomorrow after the reception?"

"Great. We could grab dinner, or..."

"Coffee would be fine. We can pick a place when we're ready to leave."

Once again she left him standing alone. This time, however, he felt as if he'd won a small victory. One step at a time, he told himself as he adjusted the weights and continued his workout.

******

"You look stunning." Selena walked around Julia, admiring the way the royal blue silk top and ivory silk pants clung to all the right places on her sister's trim figure. "Are you dressing to impress someone today?"

"Of course not. There's no one I care to impress."

"Not even Adam?"

"Especially not Adam. All I have to do is introduce him, then I'm free to enjoy my afternoon." Julia made one more turn in front of the mirror. "How about dinner afterwards?"

"Aren't you forgetting your bet with Calypso? You know, spending ten minutes with him, alone in conversation."

"Ten minutes won't be a problem."

"*Alone.*"

Julia crossed her arms, glaring at her sister. "I can do alone just fine. We'll talk about his new house." She dropped her arms to her side. "He did get his loan approved, right?"

"A quick approval. He's making a big down payment and has impeccable credit. Now he just needs to approve the inspection later this week. He may be able to move in early. I—"

They both turned at the sound of Julia's doorbell.

"Are you expecting anyone?" Selena asked.

"Maybe Calypso decided to ride with us." Julia opened the front door to see an empty porch. She stepped outside and almost tripped over a box leaning against the door jamb. "What the..."

"Who is it?"

"No one. Whoever it was left another flower box." Lifting the top off exposed a dozen lavender roses and another note, again, not signed.

"Well?" Selena glanced at the flowers before casting an expectant look at Julia.

"It says, *To a remarkable woman. I'd like to know you better.* That's it." Julia tossed the note back into the box and walked to the door, peering out one more time, seeing nothing. "This is beginning to irritate me."

Selena picked up the note, reading it through. "Well, it definitely isn't Mark, and probably not Adam—both already know you pretty well. Anyone else who's shown an interest in you?"

"No one."

"What about the developer you're working with. Didn't you say he asked you to dinner?"

"A business dinner, not a date. Besides, he wears a wedding ring." Julia pursed her lips, her brows knitting into a frown. "I hate not knowing who's sending me the flowers. Something seems so wrong about it."

Selena scooped up the flowers, grabbed a vase, and filled it with water. "Where do you want these?"

Julia looked at a vase filled with yellow roses and another with pink, irritation flowing through her once more. "Why don't you take them home? I really don't want another bouquet of anonymous flowers haunting me."

"If you're sure..."

"Definitely," she said as she checked the time. "We'd better get going."

"I heard from Selena Kerrigan you've found a house on the lake." Mayor Timmons glanced behind Adam, his eyes scanning the room as all politicians seemed born to do. "I told you those sisters are the best in town."

"Yes, sir, you did." Adam shifted from one foot to the other, wanting nothing more than to get this reception behind him so he and Julia could have the talk they'd agreed to. He'd been thinking of what he planned to say since he'd seen her in the gym.

Nine years had passed since making the biggest mistake of his life—he had to find a way to correct it. He'd replayed their Christmas Eve conversation so many times he knew it by heart. There was so much he'd change about that night if he had it to do over again. Unfortunately, being young and stupid didn't count for anything when you'd broken someone's heart.

"Hello, Thomas. Didn't expect to see you here." Timmons reached a hand out to Thomas Harten, the newest member of the City Council. "You know Adam Monroe."

"Of course. We went to high school together. Congratulations on the new job." Tom grasped Adam's hand. "I heard Julia will be making the introduction. Seems appropriate." His voice held a surprising amount of censure.

Adam tilted his head to the side, narrowing his gaze on Tom. "In what way?"

"Well, she is the president of a successful business and a force in town. She's come a long way since you dumped her."

Timmons's eyes darted from Tom to Adam, startled by the obvious contempt. "Now, Tom, that was a long time ago. Adam and Julia were young, still in their teens, as I recall. No need to bring it up now."

"Of course you're right, Mayor. Regardless, it must be quite a change for you to come back, no longer the hometown hero." Tom swallowed the last of his drink, glancing at the door. "Well, there's Julia now. Excuse me." He slipped past Adam, heading straight toward Julia.

Timmons clasped Adam on the shoulder. "Best to ignore him. His mouth always has been bigger than his ability to control it."

"No worries," Adam replied, keeping his focus on Julia. The sight of her had punched the air right out of his lungs. "Besides, everything he said is true."

"Hell, Monroe. You were kids. She may not have liked your decision, and perhaps you regret it yourself, but you can't change the past. Both of you have moved on and become successful." He waved at someone across the room. "Well, I guess I'd better work the crowd before the introductions start."

Adam watched him walk away, still aware of Julia's presence not twenty feet away. They'd moved on all right, in directions quite different than either had anticipated when they'd first left for college.

Everyone, including him, had been sure he'd excel as a pitcher in college, securing a major league deal, and spending years continuing to do what he loved since he'd first held a baseball. Julia pursued a degree in nursing, anticipating the need for a high demand job when Adam was traded between teams. They'd talked about it since their senior year in high school, planned it out the first two years of college, then he'd delivered the bomb which changed it all.

He'd heard she didn't return to college after Christmas, choosing to take a job with her father and getting a real estate license. She'd returned to school the following semester, switched her major to the business school, and never looked back.

"Now, let me bring up Julia Kerrigan, the president of our Chamber, who will make the introduction." Mayor Timmons stepped aside, letting Julia take her spot at the podium.

Adam shook his head, driving away the memories that consumed him since she arrived. It was time for him to focus on the present.

"First, I want to thank everyone for coming on a Sunday afternoon to greet our new police chief." She glanced at her notes, never making eye contact with Adam. "Many of you already know him as he was born and grew up in Peregrine Bay. He excelled as a pitcher on our state championship baseball team, then went on to obtain a degree in criminology at WSU. He's been in law enforcement since graduating, advancing through the ranks to become the youngest senior detective in Spokane's history. We are very privileged to have him back." She folded her notes and set them aside. "Without taking any more of your time, please welcome Adam Monroe, the new Police Chief of Peregrine Bay."

The crowd of about two hundred broke into enthusiastic applause as he made his way to the podium, shaking the mayor's hand. He extended his hand to Julia, but saw she'd already moved away, into the crowd, her expression unreadable.

******

Julia regretted her bet with Calypso the minute she walked into the room and spotted Adam in his uniform, filling it out better than any man should.

He'd always been handsome. Now, his taut muscles, tall stature, and magnetic presence, which had always drawn people to him, made Adam drop-dead gorgeous. She'd sucked in a nervous breath, wishing she could make a quick retreat before anyone noticed her leaving.

Instead, she scanned the room, noticing her father with a group of other men, his eyes on her. He excused himself, moving across the room in her direction as a hand touched her arm.

"Good afternoon, Julia. Looks like you had the distinct honor of introducing someone you know quite well."

She turned to see Tom Harten holding out a glass of wine and stifled a groan. "Hello, Tom. Yes, it was an honor." She turned again toward her father, who had been delayed by another conversation.

"It must be hard for you."

She shot a puzzled look at him. "What?"

"Having to introduce Adam after what he did." Tom shoved a hand in his pocket and took a sip of wine, his cocky expression turning Julia's stomach.

"Oh, that. It's not hard at all. It's been, what? Nine...ten years I believe. I never even think of it." She swallowed her wine and the lie in a big gulp, setting the empty glass on a tray. "Excuse me. I need to speak with my father."

Selena already stood by their father's side when Julia joined the small group.

"Is Joannie with you?" she asked, referring to their step-mother.

He'd married three times. His first wife followed her lover to San Francisco when Julia and Selena were young. His second wife died giving birth to Calypso. Joannie had been a nurse in the delivery room, offered to help with resources for the distraught father, and over time, became a quiet, calming force to a man too immersed in his work and grief to have the slightest idea how to handle three young daughters—one an infant. They'd married within a year and Joannie had presented him with two more girls—twins, Danielle and Lily, who were now in their final stages of college.

"She's in Boise visiting your sisters."

"I thought they were coming home for the summer. What happened?" She accepted another glass of wine from a server and took a sip, glancing over the rim at Adam, hoping he didn't notice her watching him.

"They both got jobs a couple of weeks ago. Danielle's working at a bakery near campus, and Lily is giving riding lessons and helping exercise horses at the ranch where she boards Buddy. Looks like I'll have to drive to Boise to see them. He'll do a great job."

"Who?"

"Adam. I believe the police chief job is the right fit for him." Joshua leaned over, giving her a kiss on the cheek along with a knowing smile. "Sounds like he's about done."

Now, less than five minutes later, she listened to Adam finish his remarks before turning the crowd's attention back to the mayor. *Time's up*, she thought, her heart pounding, as she faced the fact she'd have to find something to talk about with Adam.

Chapter Six

Adam milled around, waiting for Julia to finish a conversation with another of the council members. He knew all except one, a woman who moved to Peregrine Bay a few years before, didn't like the way the city was run, and won an open seat vacated by a long-time local.

From what he knew, she tended to be the one dissenting vote on most issues and was already making noises about running against the mayor in the next election. *Good luck with that*, Adam thought as he grabbed another beer from a passing server.

Julia had come up to him within minutes of the program's end, asking about his parents, his house, when he'd move in, and if he planned to hire more officers. He'd hardly get an answer out before she'd toss out another question. After a while, she left to speak with Calypso, then got hung up in the crowd. He was definitely ready to leave for their private discussion.

"How are you holding up?" Selena asked, stopping next to him.

"With this? No problem. I've done a number of community events. The difference is, most weren't attended by people who've known me most of my life." Adam nodded toward Julia. "Looks like she's going to be tied up for a while."

"Why? Do you need to speak with her?"

"We made plans to meet for coffee after the reception. Talk about some...things."

"Things, huh? Well...I wish you luck." Selena touched his arm, the look she gave him sincere.

He looked past Selena, his stomach twisting in knots, as Joshua Kerrigan walked toward them. This would be the first time he'd spoken to the elder Kerrigan since he'd tried to garner his help getting Julia back a few months after the breakup. He'd turned him down flat.

"Thought I'd come over and congratulate you, Adam. I'm certain you'll do an excellent job." He held out his hand, eyeing the man who'd been like a son to him before stunning everyone with his surprise announcement to Julia. "Must be odd being back home after all this time."

"In a way, yes. It's interesting to see how many people returned after college."

"It's a good town to raise a family. The hardest part is keeping up with the growth—schools, medical, fire stations, and police." Joshua knew the exact number of officers on the force, the total budget, arrest rate, and personal complications of most of the police staff. As one of the wealthiest citizens in the area, he made it a point to keep up with everything impacting Peregrine Bay. He'd also been the one to recommend Adam be considered for the chief position—an involvement he'd agreed to as long as his name remained confidential.

"I understand you're on the city's budget committee." Adam finished the last of his beer and set the glass aside.

"Along with a couple of council members, the mayor, and chief accountant. Let me know if you ever want to talk department numbers."

"Thank you, I'd appreciate getting together when you have time." Adam turned to see Julia moving in their direction as Joshua held out a business card.

"Here's my office number. Set something up with my assistant whenever you're ready."

"I think it went quite well," Julia said as she stopped beside her father. "And it was a great turnout. Seems everyone wants to see the old hometown hero." She cast an amused, yet dispassionate look at Adam, before glancing at her watch. "I'm beat."

"Hey, Dad. I hear you're bacheloring it tonight. How about taking me to dinner?" Selena linked an arm through her father's, casting a conspiratorial wink at Adam.

"I'd love to. You two are welcome to join us," Joshua said.

Julia's eyes darted between her father and

Adam, trying to decide what to say, not wanting to lie.

"Thank you, Mr. Kerrigan, but I have plans. It was good to see you again." Adam held up the card. "I'll set up a time to meet." He nodded to Selena, then Julia and walked out the door, heading toward his truck.

"I have plans, also. How about another time?"

"Of course, Julia. Just let me know. Ready?" he asked Selena.

She watched them leave before taking a side door, trying to avoid any prying eyes. Even though meeting with Adam wasn't a secret, a small town had a way of circulating stories that grew with each telling. She spotted him sitting in his truck.

"How private do you want this?" she asked through the open window.

"Wherever you're comfortable."

"There aren't many options on Sunday," she said, more to herself, thinking through their choices. "How about a new coffee shop north of here on the eastern edge? It's about ten minutes away."

"I'll follow you."

She pulled onto the road which circled the lake, telling herself to breathe in an attempt to settle her raging heart. The nervous sensations at being alone with him after all these years would pass after a few minutes with him, she was certain of it. They'd order coffee, say their peace, and be on their way—

within thirty minutes, tops.

All these years she'd thought of him, wondering if he enjoyed his work as a detective, if he'd met someone, fallen in love. She'd kept up with his career, been glad he'd done so well after being unable follow his dream into the major leagues.

After long days at work, she'd often pour a glass of wine and lounge in a chair, wishing she could reclaim the past, especially the way their Christmas Eve breakup turned out. By the time she realized how emotional her reaction to his request had been, it was too late. Pride overtaking common sense, she'd let him leave and never permitted another meeting.

For over four years she'd wallowed in her own misery, blaming him for everything from bad grades to lousy dates. One day she woke up, called her father, taken a few days away from her master's program, and driven to Peregrine Bay. They'd sat for the longest time, he letting her spill every detail of that night, and she listening to his wise input. She returned to school with a better understanding of what Adam had tried to do—a decision she'd been totally unprepared to accept at nineteen.

To her surprise, Joshua Kerrigan had agreed with Adam's decision, although he disapproved of the way it played out. He wanted to see his oldest daughter date others, meet new people, and make certain a life with Adam was the right choice. He'd said if the two of them were meant to be together, it would happen, and encouraged her to reach out to Adam, see if they could at least reclaim their friendship.

She'd mustered her courage, found a friend of a friend who had Adam's number, and called. What she hadn't anticipated was the female voice at the other end of the line. The woman told her Adam hadn't come home from his shift. The way she'd said *home* led Julia to believe he'd moved on, had a new life, and a new woman. Of course he would after four years. She hadn't left her name, thanked the woman, and hung up.

Tonight she'd figure out a way to deal with seeing him around town, out on dates, and eventually marrying. Her heart clenched at the thought, but it was well past time for her heart to let him go.

******

"I know we said coffee, but is dinner out of the question?" Adam asked, his stomach rumbling loud enough for them both to hear. "My treat."

She hoped to have their talk, come to some agreement on living around each other in a small town, then go home to climb into bed—alone.

"Sure. Dinner would be fine."

They ordered then talked of inconsequential

issues—the town's growth, development, the rapid expansion of her business, and his thoughts on his new job.

It was odd. As the conversation progressed, she began to think of him as a friend she'd lost touch with and now had a chance to know again. The thought lessened the tension, her hands no longer trembled, and her voice sounded calm.

Adam dug into his food as soon as it arrived, while Julia picked at hers, watching him, thinking about the number of times she'd dreamed of them having a simple meal together and talking about their day.

"How are your parents?"

He set down his fork and sat back. "They're doing well. You know they've been in Pine Cove for a while now. My dad bought a bait and tackle shop on the lake, and mom works part-time in the store." His mouth tilted up at the corners as he spoke. "I think he uses as much bait fishing as he sells."

"I saw them once a few years ago at the hardware store and said hello. They looked happy, asked about my family. You know, the usual questions." She took another bite of her salad and a sip of iced tea, wanting to ask the question that had been burning in her mind since she'd first seen him. She didn't.

"About me being back in town. I don't want what happened between us to interfere with your work or mine. You've worked hard to build your company, and I intend to make Peregrine Bay my last stop." He leaned forward, settling his forearms on the table. "I want to know if there's any chance we can be friends."

Adam had always been direct.

"Friends..." Her voice trailed off as she considered what would normally be an innocuous request. Coming from Adam, it seemed full of all kinds of complications, not to mention potential pain. Keeping their distance, showing mutual respect, and ignoring each other's personal lives seemed like a better solution than attempting to recover a friendship lost long ago.

"I can try, but I'll make no promises."

He sat back, folding his hands in his lap, and stretched out his long legs, waiting to see if she'd continue. She pursed her lips, letting her tongue skim over them, a nervous reaction he'd seen many times in the past. He knew she was thinking, deciding what to say next.

She pinned him with a direct stare, her voice steady. "I've missed you, Adam. We were friends long before we became lovers. I think that may have been the hardest part of you deciding to date. I believed we couldn't continue to be friends after being so close for so long. Losing our friendship was devastating at nineteen." She rolled her glass between her hands as if the movement helped her to focus.

Her honesty stunned him. The only thing keeping him from letting his surprise show was his training as an interrogator. He needed something stronger than coffee.

"I called you a few years ago." Her voice remained steady, resolute.

"I didn't get a message or I would've called you back."

"A woman answered, so…I didn't leave one." She shrugged as if he needed no other explanation.

"I see." He'd dated over the years, had a couple of live-in girlfriends. Each lasted a few months. No one had been able to fill the hole he'd created in his life. "Why did you call?"

"It was an impulsive act. As I recall, I'd just received the official notice I earned my master's degree and wanted to share it with you. Your girlfriend's voice startled me at first, until I realized what a dumb move I'd almost made—calling you after four years." She looked up, tilting her head. "Strange, huh?"

"I wish I'd been there for you, Julia. We could've celebrated."

"Right," she snorted. "You lived in Spokane, with another woman, and I lived here. No, it was best I hung up. Dad held a party for me at Flannigan's. Do you remember it?"

He nodded at the memory of the finest

restaurant in the area. They'd gone there for their prom both junior and senior years, plus after their high school graduation. He'd planned to propose to her there.

"Great food, wonderful people." She sighed. "Anyway, they closed a couple of years ago when their landlord tripled the rent. So, for anything truly special, the hotel restaurant, or the place where your reception was held today are the two choices."

They fell silent for a moment before Adam spoke up. "It didn't last you know."

She blinked a couple of times. "What didn't last?"

"The girlfriend. Moved in and out within three months. I couldn't wait for her to leave." He grinned up at her. "Another dumb move on my part."

"You've had others?"

He decided the timing wasn't right to confess his biggest mistake. They'd eventually get to it. "Oh yeah, some doozies." Adam drained his coffee cup and grabbed the check. "What about you and Mark? Is it serious?"

Her mouth twisted into a wry grin at the mention of the man she'd been dating. "He's a nice guy..."

"And?" he prompted when she didn't continue.

"No, it's not serious, although he'd like it to be. Don't misunderstand. I will meet someone perfect, fall in love, marry, and have children. It just hasn't happened yet."

"There's no doubt in my mind you're right." He wanted to be the one waiting for her at the end of the church aisle on her wedding day. He just needed time and patience.

"And you. Do you think you'll ever marry?"

"I'm certain of it." A smile broke across his face. "And it will be someone from Peregrine Bay."

Chapter Seven

Julia slapped the snooze button on the clock once more and turned over, the events of the last week rolling through her mind. She hadn't expected to see Adam so soon after their dinner on Sunday, but he'd called the following day asking if she'd have breakfast with him on Tuesday at a small place by the bay. She wasn't quite sure why, but she agreed.

He hadn't been at the restaurant when she arrived, so she took a table with a view of the bay and a swimming area popular with locals. She held her cup of coffee, sipping it and waiting for him to arrive when a swimmer emerged from the water. Her breath hitched as she recognized Adam.

He brought his hands up, draining the water from his hair, his long-sleeved white top clinging to every curve of his taut chest and ripped abs. He glanced around, then straight at her through the glass, offering a tentative smile as he waved. She placed a hand over her thudding heart before she tore her gaze away, staring into her coffee cup, realizing he'd caught her watching. Not ten minutes passed before he sauntered in, taking a seat across from her.

"Sorry I'm late. I got caught up in my swim and

lost track of time. I'm glad you waited."

She shifted in her seat, clearing her throat. "Of course. My calendar is clear this morning, so..." Her words drifted off as her gaze lingered on Adam a moment too long. No matter what she told herself, how she prepared for his presence, he was chipping away at her resolve. The ease with which he did it irritated her.

They placed their order, eating in silence for much of the meal, making small talk and catching up. He'd drained his coffee cup, refusing another refill, then leaned forward, resting his arms on the table.

"Have dinner with me. I don't care when, just say you will."

She first thought to decline, citing her schedule, social commitments or family obligations. In truth, her heart was the real reason she thought it a bad idea. Then her gaze moved up his face to lock with rich brown eyes that drew her in. The sincerity showing through them caused her to stop her reply and reconsider. *What if*...she thought, and found herself accepting.

A few days later, she found herself overcome by second thoughts, the butterflies in her stomach refusing to leave. She picked up the phone more than once to cancel, then thought better of it. It had been nine years, they were both older, more mature, yet neither had found anyone to replace the other. If she walked away now, she'd never know if they could reclaim what they'd lost. For the first time, she found herself seriously considering giving into her heart and allowing herself the chance for happiness.

He picked her up after work, driving to a restaurant north of Peregrine Bay. A few minutes out of town, he reached over and took her hand, grinning to himself when she didn't pull away. Instead, she slid toward him a few inches, not taking her eyes from the road.

He'd reserved a table on the outside deck with a view of the lake.

"I've never been here. What do you recommend?" Julia scanned the menu, spotting several items she'd like to try.

"Mom and Dad brought me here last week to celebrate the new job. Mom raved about the salmon, and, as you'd expect, Dad liked the rib eye."

"And you?" She glanced up over her menu, reaching for a slice of bread.

"The grilled chicken and wild mushrooms. In fact, I think I'll have it again."

She laughed as he flipped the menu closed, reaching across the table for her hand. Once more she let her fingers entwine with his, the feeling nostalgic, like coming home.

"Your hand is freezing," he said as he pushed his chair back and took the one next to her. He took each hand in turn, using both of his to rub heat into them. "We can move to inside if you'd like."

"And lose this view? Not a chance." She didn't actually care about the view. What she wanted was for him to stay next to her, inches away, with his arm draped across the back of her chair.

They talked of places they'd been, where they hoped to travel, until their words stalled at the mention of the future. Adam set down his dessert fork, pushed back the plate and turned toward Julia, his jaw working as he leaned forward, his thumb rubbing across her lower lip.

"You missed a bite," he said as he held out his thumb, then brought it to his lips, tasting the sweet tang of lemon.

She watched his movements, unaware her lips had parted, her tongue peeking out to moisten them.

He cupped her face in his hands, letting his gaze wander over her face to the fullness of her mouth, then to her deep green eyes. "I want you in my future. No other woman...just you." He leaned forward, touching his lips with hers before delivering a searing kiss that sent tremors through both of them. The beginning of a devastating grin tipped the corners of his mouth up as he pulled back. "We don't need to talk more of it tonight. I just didn't want you leaving here without knowing how I feel."

He'd driven her home, kissing her lightly, asking if he could see her again soon. All she could do was nod, causing a crooked smile to brighten his face.

She'd lain awake for hours rehashing Adam's words the night before, words that curled around her heart, squeezing out the small amount of resistance still left. There now remained no doubt in her mind he wanted her. In all the years she'd known him, he'd never lied to her. She might not have liked what he said, but lying held no place in his life.

Julia touched her lips with a finger, closing her eyes, remembering the sensations of his touch. No man had ever affected her the way he did and she doubted anyone ever would.

She groaned at the thought, turned off the alarm, dragged herself out of bed, and headed for the shower, remembering his comment a week before about being certain he'd find the right person to marry in Peregrine Bay.

At the time, she thought he meant someone else, one of several women who remained single and lived in town. Now she wasn't so certain.

Images of female classmates rolled across her mind as she shampooed her long hair. Not one seemed his type. Then again, she no longer had any idea what attracted him. She almost laughed. If she were to believe him, his type hadn't changed—he still wanted her. She shuddered at the thought as she turned off the shower, grabbed a towel, and stepped into the bedroom to the sound of her phone.

"Hello." She adjusted the phone to her other ear when she got no response. "Hello," she repeated twice more before hanging up.

Thirty minutes later she poured coffee and read the paper, seeing a brief article on a new business, an announcement of another closing, and a schedule of activities for the opening of a new park. Her stomach fluttered as she thought of inviting Adam to sit with her family at the annual barbecue.

She reached over to grab the phone as it rang a second time. "Hello." Again she heard no response. "Hello," she said with more force, knowing someone was at the other end. "Look, whoever you are, please stop calling. It's wasting your time and mine."

Grabbing her purse, she walked into the garage and slid inside her car before noticing a package wrapped in plain paper on the passenger seat. It appeared to be about the size of a coffee table picture book, and as she picked it up, noted it felt just as heavy.

Julia tore off the wrapping to find a class yearbook from her senior year, unsigned, with little wear. She thumbed through it, noticing the lack of signatures or comments common when friends passed their books around. Finding the senior class photos, she searched for Adam's picture, then gasped when she found it.

A red 'x' had been drawn across his face, a handwritten note below it.

He was never good enough for you, also in red ink.

Her hands began to shake as she thumbed to her own photo, one word scrawled across it.

Mine.

Julia tossed the book back onto the seat, wondering how someone had entered a garage with an electronic roll-up door. She always left her car inside and unlocked, but a deadbolt with a keypad secured the back entry door and she'd installed locks on the window.

Julia thought of the flowers, a slight shiver running through her as she speculated on the chance all of this was just a coincidence. He father would say 'no,' and she tended to agree. She just didn't know what to do. There were no threats and no one seemed to be following her, yet she felt as if she were being stalked.

She dashed inside, grabbed the notes that accompanied the flowers, then got back in her car, hurrying toward the other flower shop in town.

******

A bell jingled overhead as she walked inside

Bayside Floral. It appeared to be about twice the size of the other shop with shelves featuring gifts, pottery, and candles as well as pre-arranged bouquets.

"May I help you?" A middle aged woman with short black hair walked out, wiping her hands down her apron.

"I hope so. It's a bit of a strange request. You see, I've been receiving flowers from an anonymous sender—lavender, pink, yellow—all roses. I wondered if you might remember someone ordering them or recognize these cards."

"Let me check the sales log." She pulled up a sales report and stared at her computer screen. "I have several orders of a dozen of all three colors being sold over the last ten days. Most paid with credit cards."

"Can you tell if the same customer placed three separate orders?"

She studied the screen again. "One person bought a dozen pink and another dozen lavender using a credit card. There are several cash payments, so I can't tell if it's the same person or not as most don't provide their names. Were these delivered to your home or office?"

"Both. Two were left outside my front door at home." Julia slipped the cards back in her purse.

"It's probably some shy admirer of yours. I'll do my best to keep watch for anyone buying roses and paying with cash. Since I've been open less than a year, I still see a lot of unfamiliar faces. Wish I could be of more help."

"You've been wonderful. Thanks."

Julia climbed into her car, deciding she needed to speak to one other person about the flowers.

******

"Here you go, Chief."

Adam took the package from the officer at the front desk and disappeared into his office, setting the parcel aside. He checked for voice messages and read the few emails waiting for him, then grabbed a cup of coffee, knowing it would be a long day. He had a meeting with the mayor in an hour, another with the county sheriff afterwards, a staff meeting in the afternoon, and one with the district attorney before he'd be able to settle down and study the budget for his meeting later in the week with Joshua Kerrigan.

He turned toward the file cabinet behind him, ignoring the sound of the front entrance door as it opened and closed.

"Good morning, Ms. Kerrigan. Are you here to see the chief?"

Adam shifted back around, surprised and pleased to see Julia staring at him.

"Yes. If he's available."

"I believe you can see that I am. Come on back." He wanted to pull her close, kiss her senseless, but desire gave way to professionalism. "Have a seat while I clear away this stuff." He moved piles of paper and files, then sat down at his desk.

"I hope I'm not interrupting anything." She scanned the room, seeing a couple of pictures of Adam with his parents and another with his two brothers and sister.

"Not at all. Is this a personal visit or business?" He hoped it might be personal given the way their evening the night before had ended. Then he noticed the way her brows knit together.

"Business...I think."

"All right. Talk to me."

"First, I need to ask if you sent me any flowers since you've been back."

"No, I haven't." He sat forward, leaning his arms on the table. "When I saw you in the floral shop, I assumed Mark sent them to you."

"No, he didn't." She explained as best she could, showing him the cards and describing the phone calls. "So I have this mystery person sending me flowers, someone calling and not saying a word, and now a package placed on the seat of my car." She glanced at his desk. "In fact, it looked quite similar to the one on your desk."

"This one?" he asked, nodding toward the package he'd been handed not fifteen minutes before. Adam didn't like where this seemed to be heading. He slipped on evidence gloves, picked up the package, and tore off the wrapper, exposing a yearbook.

Julia sucked in a breath. "My God, that's just like the one I got. Open it up to your picture."

His gaze narrowed on her, but he did as she asked, turning to the location of his senior photo.

"Did yours look like this?" He turned the book around, showing her a picture of him with a red 'x' across his face with wording beside it.

"Yes." She leaned forward to get a better look.

You never were good enough for her.

"Adam..." she breathed out, "mine said almost the same. Now, turn to my photo."

He did, muttering an oath when he saw what was written beside it.

She's mine.

"What's it say?" Julia asked, standing to get a better view.

He turned it around, anger and dread swelling within him. "Is this what yours said?"

"Pretty much."

Adam stood, slipped the book into an evidence bag and grabbed an evidence collection kit. "Where's your book?"

"In my car."

"I'll put it in my truck, then follow you to your place."

******

Adam stared at the one box Julia kept. A simple blue flower container with no identifying marks as to who sent it or the floral shop. He knew of one flower shop in Pine Cove and a couple others around the lake, but felt certain whoever sent them paid with cash and didn't leave their name. He'd already bagged the yearbook, then checked for prints in the garage and around the front door, expecting to find nothing except a match to Julia and her sisters.

She held out a cup of coffee to him, then settled onto the sofa.

"What do you think?"

He sat next to her, taking her hand in his.

"Whoever is doing this has made no outright threats, although it's obvious he's trying to scare and intimidate you. He lives in the area, knows both of us, probably since high school, and believes you and I are getting back together—he wouldn't have left the messages otherwise." He squeezed her hand before pulling out a notepad and pen. "I'm going to need a list of people from high school who still live in the area, plus the names of the men you've dated since we split up."

Julia snorted, the corners of her mouth turning up. "The list of locals who went to school about the time we did will be pretty long. The other one not so much, so I'll start with it." She stood and grabbed his empty cup, setting it on the kitchen counter. "Besides Mark, I dated Jeremy Butler for a few months, Joss Gremling, and Toby Pullman."

"You dated Toby?" The look he shot her said exactly what he thought of her going out with someone everyone considered way out of her league.

She shifted toward him, pinning him with a look he couldn't quite interpret. "He's smart, a nice guy, dependable, and very funny. I hired him to take care of the technology set up and computer issues at the company."

"Then why aren't you still with him if he's such a great guy?" Adam smirked as he jotted down the names Julia tossed out.

The answer, to her, was obvious. *Because he wasn't you.* "We had fun but it was never a romantic relationship. Regardless, he took a high-paying job at a tech company in Seattle."

Adam scratched Toby off the list. "Who's Joss Gremling? Does he work in town?"

"Not any longer. He's an engineer. Travels the world doing large construction projects. I helped him find some land for a vacation home he plans to build. It was short-term, casual, and quite uncomplicated."

Again, Adam drew a line through a name. "That leaves Jeremy Butler. The name rings a bell, but I can't place him."

"I'm certain that would offend Jeremy as you played baseball with him. He joined the varsity team as a freshman during our senior year, played third base, with a batting average of over .400. He came back to town for a while after college, then left when he got a deal with the Detroit minor league system. I received a text from him a few months ago. They've moved him to the majors."

Adam's hand stilled as he took in all she said. He did remember Jeremy, a real good player with a great attitude. Someone who Julia would find attractive.

Adam hadn't thrown a ball in close to seven years, yet there were days all he could think about were missed opportunities and what he'd give for another chance at the big leagues.

"So you dated a guy four years younger than you?"

Her face broke into a broad smile. "Three years. He missed a year of school back when he was nine. Heart problems as I recall." She walked to within a foot of him. "Don't tell me you haven't dated women at least that much younger than you."

He glanced away, remembering one woman. At twenty-one, she was six years younger than him when they went out. Although there'd been no future in it, the fling had turned into a wild few weeks right before he'd been promoted to senior detective.

He ignored her comment, reviewing the list. "Just the three guys?" None sounded serious. He put on his game face, trying to hide his relief at the few men she'd dated.

She pursed her lips, trying to remember if there was anyone else. "No one else from the area."

"And outside the area?"

"That would be none of your business, Chief Monroe." She smiled, cocking an eyebrow. "So, what's next?"

Adam grinned, slapping the notebook shut, thinking they'd get back to that question later. "I'll run the prints but doubt we'll find anything. I want to speak with Tricia at your office, and anyone else who might accept deliveries. Selena and Calypso should be told what's going on so they can keep watch of people coming and going. I doubt he wants to hurt you. His intent seems to be to put a scare in you, keep us away from each other."

"That's a good point," she threw over her shoulder as she walked toward the kitchen. "If we keep a distance between us, he may give up."

He followed her, turned her toward him, running a finger down her cheek. She was right, but it was not in his plans. "Not going to happen, Julia." He intended to spend more time with her, not less.

She stepped away as heat strummed through her at his light touch. "I need to leave for the office.

Is there anything else?" Julia slung her purse over her shoulder.

"Let me see your security system before you leave."

She blinked a couple of times. It was one of the items still on her growing list of stuff to get done.

"I don't have one."

"An attractive, prominent, single woman, living alone outside of town needs a security system. I'll call a friend of mine and get him out here tonight. If you can't be here, I'll meet with him."

She pulled out her phone and checked her schedule. "I'll be here. Let me know when."

"I'll be here also."

"There's no need—"

"It's not a problem. I want to talk with them about my house anyway."

She started to respond when her phone rang. "Hello." She waited a moment before repeating her greeting, then muttered a curse, holding the phone toward Adam and whispering, "Same thing. Calls, but doesn't respond."

Adam grabbed the phone, noting no caller I.D. appeared. "Who is this?" he growled. "Whoever you are, take my advice and stay away from Julia..." his voice trailed off as the caller hung up. "I want you to get a record of incoming calls on your phone. You should be able to download it online. Identify any you don't recognize."

"Wouldn't he block it?"

"Probably, but we need to check anyway." This time his phone rang. "Monroe." He listened a moment. "I'll be there in fifteen minutes." He glanced at Julia. "I've got to leave. I'll let you know when the security company will be here." Adam opened the door then turned back to her. "Keep watch, Julia. We can't assume this guy isn't a threat."

Chapter Eight

"Have a seat, Chief Monroe. The mayor will be with you in a few minutes."

He'd lost track of time while at Julia's, missing the original appointment by over an hour. As far as he knew, the mayor had nothing pressing—at least that's what Adam hoped.

"You can go in now."

Adam walked into the office, noting the scowl on the mayor's face. "Apologies, Mayor. A situation came up I had to take care of."

"I heard you left the office with Julia Kerrigan. Personal business is no excuse for missing our meeting."

"She came in to lodge a complaint about someone harassing her. Wasn't much I could do except go check it out."

The mayor's expression changed at Adam's explanation. "What's going on with Julia?"

"Seems someone may have fixated on her. Sending flowers with a message but no name, calling but not speaking, leaving a package in her car—"

"Doesn't she lock it?"

"It was parked in her garage."

The mayor let out a whispered expletive.

"I couldn't see how he got inside. She has combination locks on all her outside doors and swears no one has the code except family. Right now, I believe she's more irritated than afraid."

"What do you think?"

Adam explained the packages they'd both received, how Julia had already spoken with both the florists in town, and the last call before he'd left her home.

"Sounds to me as if this has been brewing for some time. My arrival triggered his actions as I must assume he doesn't want us back together."

"Is there a chance of that?"

Adam fingered the brim of his hat, contemplating how much to say. He knew the mayor to be a distant relation to the Kerrigan family with a particular fondness for Julia.

"Perhaps."

"Well, you just hang in there." The mayor's chuckle caught Adam by surprise. After what happened, he assumed no one associated with the Kerrigans would ever want to see them reunited. "You let me know if there's anything I can do on this. Joshua will be mighty upset if this goes any further."

Adam nodded. "If there's nothing else…"

"There is one other item, which is why I wanted to meet with you. The rodeo is coming to town in

July and you've been selected as the Grand Marshal for the parade."

Adam groaned. All he wanted was to do his job. "I don't—"

"Now I know you don't like being in the spotlight. The problem is, you were the selection of both the City Council and the Rodeo Committee. Hell, Adam, it's an honor. Enjoy it."

"Fine." He stood and slammed his hat on his head. "If that's it, I'll get back to the office and the Kerrigan case."

The mayor waved him off, already picking up the phone.

******

"Thanks, Dad. I'll be sure and let Selena know." Julia hung up then opened her email, scanning the latest messages. One, in particular, caught her attention, with a subject line stating it was urgent. She didn't recognize the sender, but opened it anyway, her jaw dropping as she read it.

I have pictures of what you did. Stay away from Monroe or I'll post them so all can see.

Her hand came up to her throat as her heart thundered in her chest. She tried to wrap her mind around the message and its implication she'd done something illegal or immoral. Whatever this person had must be devastating or they wouldn't threaten its release.

She thought through her business dealings, personal relationships, and civic activities, coming up with nothing that could be considered illegal, and certainly nothing immoral. Her love life was a joke. She'd been scrupulous about the men she dated since Adam, taking no chances of getting hurt again. No married men, not even men who'd been through a recent breakup. At this point, no one knew she and Adam were seeing each other on a casual basis. Sex pretty much consisted of the battery operated gizmo Calypso had given her a few years ago when Julia had let slip the length of time since she'd slept with a man.

She believed most thought her relationship with Mark had turned intimate. It hadn't, and given her feelings, never would. Deep down, Julia believed she lacked something. If not, Adam wouldn't have walked away, leaving her with a crushing sense of insecurity.

There'd been two men since Adam. The first one had been a disaster. The second, uninspiring.

She reached for the phone as another email popped up from a different sender. The subject line read *take a look*. Her hand shook as she opened the message, watching as an image opened bit-by-bit, until she knew without doubt, what it showed.

Julia drew in a sharp breath as her phone began to ring. She answered, not able to take her gaze off the image.

"Hello..." she breathed out.

"It's Adam. We have a meeting at seven tonight with the security company."

"Can you come to my office? I, uh..."

He could hear the tension in her voice laced with fear. "I'll be right there."

Julia hung up, closing the message, and burying her face with her hands.

******

Adam dashed into the office, ignoring Tricia as he opened Julia's door, seeing her stare at her computer screen.

"Chief Monroe, you—"

"It's all right, Tricia. I asked him to come."

Adam pulled the door closed, not liking the ghost white appearance of Julia's face or the way her lower lip trembled. "What is it?" He walked up to her, leaning over, draping an arm across her shoulders while glancing at the screen.

She clicked the message, letting the photo reappear.

Adam watched as an image of the two them, making love, filled the screen. His hand clasped her shoulder as he murmured an oath. She scrolled further and another image appeared, this one more explicit, with a clear view of each face.

She looked up at him, her face ashen. "What are we going to do? He's threatened to make these public."

He twisted her chair around, grasping her shoulders, and pulling her up to him. She wrapped her arms around his waist, resting her head on his chest as she tried to control the panic pulsing through her.

"Julia, look at me." He lifted her chin with a finger, his face calm, reassuring. "We did nothing wrong. We were young and in love." His hand splayed across her back, moving up and down in a soothing motion. "The person who took these and sent them to you is the one who's sick." He locked his gaze with hers, trying to control the anger surging through him. "We will find whoever is doing this and stop him."

He could feel her arms tighten around him, her body shaking as she let her forehead rest once again on his chest. His chin lowered to the top of her head. Adam closed his eyes, loving the feel of her body aligned with his after all these years. He knew those thoughts were out of line, especially now. But God help him, he wanted her with a craving he'd never been able to crush.

"Do you recognize who sent this?"

"No."

"All right, we'll shut down your computer and take it to the station. There's an expert I can bring in to track where the message came from, and with luck, who sent it."

She looked up. "I don't want anyone to see them."

"I'll do everything I can to keep the number of eyes on this to just those who must have access. You'll have to trust me." He placed a soft kiss on her forehead before stepping away.

******

Julia paced back and forth in her living room as she and Adam waited for the security technician to arrive. They'd secured her computer at the police station pending the arrival of the computer expert the following day. Adam wanted to use someone he knew in Spokane, a person without any connection to Peregrine Bay. A man he could trust to keep his mouth shut.

She stopped at the window and swiveled back to face him. "You're certain he's the best for this? I can get Toby—"

"And have him see those pictures of us. Not a chance."

Julia crossed her arms and bit her lower lip.

"We'll use Vic. If he fails to identify the person, we'll try someone else. And, I'm staying here tonight."

She started to say something then closed her

mouth when the doorbell rang. "We're not finished with this conversation," she said, opening the door.

"Good evening. I'm Deke Costanza with Templar Security."

"Come on in. I'm Julia Kerrigan and this is Police Chief Monroe."

"Sorry the boss couldn't be here. I guess you heard he's out of town." He shook their hands while looking around. "Why don't you show me the house and we'll go from there."

An hour later they'd agreed on a system and price. Deke had Julia sign the agreement then arranged to have the installation team return the following day.

"I'll let you know if there's any delay. The boss said you also need a system for your place. Is it okay if we meet there later this week?" he asked Adam.

"Let me call you. I need to get access since the deal hasn't closed yet."

"Gotcha. Just let me know."

Julia closed the door behind Deke then whipped around to stare at Adam. "I'm not certain it's such a good idea for you to stay the night."

"On the sofa. You'll never know I'm here." Adam stood and pulled out his car keys. "I'm pulling the cruiser into the garage. If he does come back tonight, I don't want him to see it."

She thought of locking the door behind him, then reconsidered and opened the garage door to allow him access. It surprised her how disappointed she felt when he'd offered to sleep on the couch.

It seemed almost surreal having him so close, yet feeling an invisible barrier separating them. Although she'd long ago come to accept that his decision to date was sound, she hadn't arrived at the point of admitting it—or letting him know how much she regretted not allowing him to explain. The time they'd spent together since his return opened all the old wounds even as it gave her hope they could work it out, perhaps build a life. He'd take the next step if she'd give him the opportunity—she just needed to decide if she had the courage to open her heart to him again.

"You know, if the person harassing me finds out you're here, it just might trigger him to release the pictures across the Internet," she said as he walked in from the garage.

He tossed his keys on a table as he kept moving forward, not stopping until he stood inches from her, crowding her space. She tried stepping backward, stopping when she bumped into the edge of a chair. He didn't make any move to touch her as his eyes searched her face.

"I'm staying because I'm worried about you. And because you want me to."

"That's not true." She crossed her arms, doing her best to glower at him. Although the tactic worked on many people, it never had on Adam.

"Right. And if I walked out that door, how would you feel?"

"Glad."

He stepped closer, letting a finger trail down her cheek, seeing the slight shiver at his action. "You're sure that's how you'd feel?" He let his finger move lower, down the column of her neck to the top of her blouse.

Even though she steeled herself against his touch, her breath caught as her feelings for him demanded release. She fisted her hands at her sides, let out a groan then stepped aside.

Chapter Nine

"Don't, Adam. I can't do this with you. Not again." She kept stepping away until six feet separated them. "I think you should leave," she whispered.

"I'm not leaving tonight, Julia. At least not until we've had a chance to talk."

She swallowed the lump in her throat, not wanting to revisit the past. "About what?"

"The mess I made of our lives. The way we left it, with both of us feeling crushed."

"You, crushed? That's not how I remember the night. You broke it off because you'd met someone else. What we had wasn't good enough for you, so you bailed. It appears that didn't work out for you." Her voice rose as her anger spiked. She wanted to pound her fists into his chest, rage at him for all the hurt he'd caused, then wrap her arms around him and never let go. Her head ached at the mixed feelings battling within her.

Adam shredded both hands through his short hair and closed his eyes, knowing everything she said was right, and hating himself for all of it. He dropped his arms to his sides, palms out.

"No, it didn't work out. I never thought it would. She was not the reason I wanted space...time to be certain we were making the right decision for the rest of our lives. I planned to marry one time, and I needed to be certain. Hell, Julia, we were nineteen. I didn't want to go through what my parents did, talking divorce after twenty years. I needed to be sure." He turned away from her, pacing several feet away and shoving his hands in his pockets.

She took a few steps forward, not getting too close. "But your parents didn't get a divorce."

He turned toward her, letting his gaze fall to the floor. "You never knew, but my mother called, asking that I come home a day earlier, on December 23. I'll never forget that day...or the following." He glanced up at her. "I walked into the house to see a stack of boxes and suitcases by the front door, my dad beginning to load them into the back of his truck. I knew they were having problems—we'd talked about it at Thanksgiving. That's when I learned my dad hadn't been ready to marry when they found out Mom was pregnant...with me. They were nineteen. I just couldn't get the conversation out of my mind. When I went back to school after Thanksgiving, I decided to go out with a girl who'd been dogging me for months. I just wanted to figure things out."

"The cheerleader..." she breathed out, lowering herself to the sofa.

"Someone told you about her?"

"Yes. There were people who couldn't wait to tell me how you'd moved on." She gripped her hands together until her knuckles were almost white.

"I'm sorry, Julia. It wasn't my intention to hurt you. I knew, even then, it wouldn't work with her. I didn't think it would work with anyone but you. When my mom called and I got home for Christmas, saw what my parents were going through, I decided we did need the time to date other people, make sure what we felt had a chance to last." He rested against a table, taking a breath, and shaking his head. "Mom and Dad worked through their problems. He moved out for a couple months. Both were miserable. They just had to go through the split to be sure."

She rested her elbows on her knees and lowered her head into her hands, all the hurt ripping through her again as if the breakup happened days instead of years ago.

"I knew within a few months you were the one. No doubt. By then, you wouldn't accept my calls, return emails, and your father refused to let me see you when I came home. I screwed it all up, Julia. You'll never know how sorry I am for losing you." He slumped onto the sofa, defeat like he hadn't known in years washing over him.

Julia wrapped her arms around her waist and tried to absorb all he'd said. She'd had some good years, done well in business, felt like a success. No one knew how alone she felt, how no one ever filled the void Adam created.

"I'm a lousy date," she stated in a calm voice.

He looked over at her. "What's that?"

"Dating. I'm horrible at it." She shook her head. "I've had less than a dozen dates...most were miserable."

"I heard you had a couple boyfriends."

She snorted. "One lasted two months and another less than that. Not what I'd call a success story. Now you, I heard all kinds of stories of parties, beautiful coeds, live-in girlfriends. It sounded like you didn't stumble at all."

"I broke it off with the first girl within a couple of months then fell flat on my face. About a year later, when I finally accepted you'd never let me explain or see you again, I did begin to go out. Not one girl I dated seemed right. At first, all they saw was a star college pitcher. They didn't want me...they wanted the parties and spotlight. The injury to my arm during senior season made me take stock of everything. Graduating, being accepted into the police academy gave me purpose, and I enjoyed the work. I also found out how much women like a man in uniform—any uniform. I worked hard and played harder. Still, all I felt when I came home was hollow and empty inside. My apartment became a place to sleep before starting the routine all over again. Do you want to know why I accepted the job here?"

Did she? She wasn't sure. "Yes."

"You're why I'm here. I knew you'd never married, and, well…I needed to see if there was a chance you'd ever forgive me, allow us to have another chance."

Elation warred with common sense, and dread. He'd said almost the same words at dinner, and she'd had the same reaction. She never thought they'd have another chance. Now he offered her the opportunity she'd dreamed about since the day he left. He sat a few feet away, a look of hope mingled with regret on his face. She needed to decide if fear or hope would rule her decision.

She dropped her arms from around her waist and pushed from the chair, her inner turmoil becoming unbearable, knowing what she wanted and needing the courage to reach out for it. "Wine, beer…water?"

"A beer would be great." He joined her in the kitchen, feeling awkward and unsure.

She handed him a bottle, poured her wine, and took a sip, letting the cool liquid bathe her throat. Resting against the counter, she turned toward him.

"It's been a long time, Adam, and we've changed so much."

"Not so much as you think." He tipped back the bottle, taking a long swallow.

"You wanted to pitch in the majors. Instead you're the chief of police in your hometown. I wanted to be a nurse, but I run a real estate firm—"

"In the same small town." He set the bottle down. "Let me ask you something. Are you happy with your work, enjoy going in each day?"

"Yes, I love it. And you?"

"I believe it's what I was always meant to do. Baseball was great, but an injury disrupted my plans." He reached for her hand, grasping it in his as he rubbed his thumb in circles. "Sometimes stuff happens we can't figure out. After a while, it begins to make sense, even turning into something better than what we'd planned."

She studied their joined hands, remembering other times he'd held it in the exact same way, then pulled her to him, kissing her until they were both breathless. This time he didn't draw her in as if waiting for an invitation.

"I never stopped loving you. All I'm asking for is another chance. If it doesn't work out, I'll accept it and leave you alone with no regrets."

"You'd stay in town, keep your job?"

"I would. I'd just have to live with the knowledge you'd meet someone else, marry, and be lost to me forever." He exhaled, shifting his body closer to hers. "I wouldn't like it, but I'd learn to accept it."

She began to lean into him when a noise on the

front porch had Adam dropping her hand as he dashed to the door, Julia a few feet behind. They'd left a light on, and unless someone came by earlier, no one except his office knew he was there. He motioned for her to stay behind him as he pulled his service revolver and pulled the door open.

"Grab that." He motioned to an envelope, scanned the area in front of her house, then took off at a run toward the sound of a car engine firing up.

He slowed as headlights appeared across the main road, not fifteen feet from where he stood.

"Stop," he ordered, holding his gun in front of him, noticing a male driver and no passenger.

The car began to inch forward before the driver glanced outside to see the barrel of a gun pointed his way. He turned off the engine and rolled down the window.

"Something I can do for you, Officer?"

"Put your hands on the steering wheel where I can see them." Adam took several steps forward as the driver complied, never taking his eyes off him, a sudden burst of recognition registering. "Mr. Farrell?" he asked, not lowering his weapon.

"Adam Monroe. I thought that was you." Farrell began to lower his hands until a command from Adam stopped him.

"Leave your hands on the wheel. I'll open the door so you can get out." He stepped to the car, glanced inside, noticing a notebook on the passenger seat, a jacket in the back, and nothing else. "All right, step on out."

"What's going on here?" Farrell's voice remained steady, his eyes assessing Adam.

"Turn around and place your hands on the hood."

"What the—"

"Do as I ask, Mr. Farrell, then I'll explain." Adam patted him down and holstered his gun, while taking a quick look behind him. He could see Julia standing on the front porch and motioned her to stay put. "All right, you can turn around and explain to me why you're parked on the side of the road outside Ms. Kerrigan's house."

Farrell glared at him before his face turned from anger to interest. "I had a call to make, so I pulled over. Why? Is Julia in some kind of trouble?"

"There's been some disturbances around her place and she asked me to check them out."

"What kind of disturbances?" He peered around Adam, trying to see Julia.

"The harassing kind. We heard a noise on the porch, saw an envelope had been left, so I decided to check it out and found you starting your engine. Is there a reason you chose this particular spot to park?" Adam had known Mr. Farrell since he and Julia had taken high school science from him. Slim and unassuming, he didn't seem the type to harass anyone, yet Adam chose to be cautious. A stalker could be anyone as he'd discovered while working as a detective.

He waved his hand toward the shoulder of the road. "As you can see, there's a little more room to pull off here than on most of this road. Nothing nefarious, Adam, I can assure you."

Something about the way Farrell kept glancing behind Adam had him on alert, even though the explanation made sense.

"How long have you been parked?"

"Not long. Maybe two minutes."

"Did you see anyone when you pulled over? Another car, a person?"

"Now that you mention it, I did see someone walking on the other side of the road as I stopped. I didn't pay much attention. He was heading toward town."

"Can you describe him?"

"I'm afraid not. He wore dark colors, that's all I remember."

"Well, if you think of anything else, here's my card. I'd appreciate it if you'd call me."

Farrell dropped the card into a pocket. "Well, it was good to see you, Adam, even under these circumstances."

Adam stepped aside as Farrell got in his car and pulled away. He continued to watch as the taillights disappeared around a corner before returning to the house.

"Who was that?" Julia asked, meeting him on the porch.

"Mr. Farrell."

"You're kidding? Why would he be parked there?"

He ushered her inside and closed the door, spotting the envelope on the table. "That's a good question. He says he pulled over to make a call and happened to do it across the street from your house."

"Just a coincidence, I guess."

Adam had come to believe less and less in coincidences during his time as a cop, yet their former high school science teacher harassing Julia seemed a stretch. He picked up the envelope, noticing Julia hadn't opened it. He glanced at her.

"Go ahead and open it. Might as well see what he left this time." She leaned toward him, bracing herself for what would be inside.

"More pictures." He drew them out, looking at each and muttering a curse before holding them out toward Julia. "You don't have to look at these. They're more of the same night."

She looked from him to the photos, taking a breath before reaching out her hand. One by one she shuffled through them, her hands shaking, seeing their entire session played out on film, from the time they parked Adam's truck in the dense trees near the lake until they dressed and drove away. She felt a wave of nausea at the thought others might be able to see what they'd done.

"What will we do? He must know you were here tonight. What if he releases them, puts them on the Internet or sends them to the mayor, or council, or...?" Her voice cracked as the ramifications of their action as teenagers hit her full force.

Adam grabbed her by the shoulders and drew her to him, wrapping his arms around her, resting his chin on the top of her head.

"Mayor Timmons and the others know we were close in high school. Even though I don't want anyone to see them, I doubt they'll be surprised to know what we did. It would be embarrassing for both of us, but nothing more."

"But they're so graphic, so..." she stopped, swiping away a tear escaping down her cheek, panic threatening to overwhelm her.

"Yes, they're graphic, but also a reflection of how we felt about each other. It's as if someone invaded our bedroom, making something dirty out of what was beautiful." He skimmed a hand down her hair, wrapping it around the back of her neck, gently kneading the tense muscles. "You're exhausted. Go to bed. We'll figure this out in the morning." He leaned back, tilted her head up, and placed a kiss on her lips.

He began to pull away before she gripped his arms tighter, drawing him to her.

Chapter Ten

The images of the two of them together flashed through Julia's mind as she settled her mouth on his and deepened the kiss, not wanting to let go, yet not knowing where tonight would lead. The thought of others seeing the pictures scared her, but the photos also did something else.

As she'd stared at the two of them together, for the first time, she saw herself as Adam saw her, filled with passion, wanting him with every fiber of her being, a woman consumed with desire. The knowledge rocked her.

She'd always thought it her fault making love with others had been a disaster. The photos told a different story. It had been the men, not her.

Adam was who she wanted, still loved, and who could bring out the passion she concealed within her. No one else.

Her hands moved up to his shoulders and wrapped around his neck, drawing him down. Her tongue traced the fullness of his lips, before he took over, exploring the recesses of her mouth. She relaxed, giving in to the hunger she felt for the man in her arms. Her hands moved down his back, feeling the wall of muscles under his uniform.

Pulling his shirt free, Julia explore him, skin-to-skin, until heat coursed through her. She couldn't get close enough as their kisses became almost frenzied and Adam pulled free, looking down on her with glazed eyes.

"What do you want, Julia?" His lips brushed against hers as he spoke, his voice hoarse with desire.

"You, Adam. I want you."

He drew away, wanting her with an intensity he'd felt for no other woman. Yet, he sensed the need for caution. "This isn't a good idea...not tonight." He placed a tender kiss on her lips. "You're upset about what's happening and may regret this when you have time to think it through. I want you, but not as a response to what's going on."

She placed her hands on his face, searching his eyes, seeing all she needed.

"No, this is about us. What we had and lost. I want it back, with you, tonight." She drew him down to her for a kiss that had them both moaning.

Without another word, he swept her into his arms and carried her to the bedroom, settling her on the bed before stripping off his shirt and stretching out beside her. He traced a finger down her cheek, settling his hand on the top button of her blouse.

"Understand, Julia, if we do this, it isn't for one night. I can't have one night then let you go."

She grasped his hand with hers and brought it to her lips. "I know."

******

Adam struggled with fatigue, the phone's ring wakening him from one of the best nights he'd had since...*Julia*. He glanced down to see her stretched across his chest, a leg thrown over his thigh. He'd never seen anything more beautiful or felt more at peace in his life.

He ignored the phone, tightening his hold on her, careful not to let her wake.

One time had turned to two, then three before neither could hold off sleep any longer. Now he wanted her again. He stroked a hand up her back, his heart pounding at the memory of the night before. In his mind, there would be no going back. She was his again, and there was nothing he wouldn't do to keep her.

She began to stir as the phone rang again. This time he slid from beneath her and grabbed it.

"Monroe."

"Chief, this is Officer Olander."

"Yes, Olander. What do you need?" He glanced at Julia, wanting to crawl back under the covers with her and continue.

"There's a pretty bad situation here you need to know about."

Adam's chest tightened, sensing he knew what was coming. "Go on."

"We received an envelope addressed to you and all interested parties." Olander cleared his throat. "I didn't think much of it and opened it. Two other officers were standing behind me when I did, and...I'm not sure how to tell you this."

"They're of Julia Kerrigan and me, together. Right?"

"Yes, sir, they are, and they're pretty graphic."

Adam worked to calm his breathing and his rage. He had to be in control.

"Are you aware of the harassment case we're checking in to?"

"Yes, sir. Ms. Kerrigan has filed complaints. I assume this is part of it."

"It is. He left a similar set of photographs at her home last night. Who else knows about this?"

"Just myself and the two other officers. Both are good people and won't say anything until you have a chance to fill us in. But, Chief, there's something else."

"What is it?"

"A note inside."

"Read it to me."

"Peregrine Bay police chief engaging in underage sex."

"Shit," Adam growled. "I'll be there within half an hour." He hung up, glancing at Julia to see her propped up on one arm, staring at him, eyes wide. He slipped into his shirt and pants, then sat on the edge of the bed, taking her hand in his. "The same set of photos is at the police station." He put his arms around her, pulling her close as a gasp escaped her lips. "For now, I can control who sees them, but that won't last." He bent down and kissed her. "I need to go and handle damage control. Will you be all right?"

She took a shaky breath, closing her eyes at the turmoil now ruling her life. "Yes. Do you need me to come by the station?" She pushed herself away, pulling the covers around her and brushing the hair from her face.

"No. What I need is for you to go about your day, acting like nothing out of the ordinary has happened. Have you talked with Selena and Calypso yet?" He stood, buttoning his shirt, and tying his shoes.

"Yes, but they know nothing of the pictures, and I don't want to discuss it with them."

He understood her reluctance, but sometimes the best way to combat a bully was to outmaneuver them.

"I think you need to be prepared to address it with them. We don't know who this lunatic is and can't do anything about it until we identify him. Will you be at your office?"

Julia nodded, dreading what she might find

when she arrived.

"Look, I'll come by and take you to lunch. We can talk more about it then."

Adam began to leave then walked back to the bed and leaned over, giving her one more kiss, wanting it to be more. "I'm staying here tonight. Any objections?"

Julia wrapped her arms around his neck, giving him one more lingering kiss before pulling back. "No objections at all."

******

"Where have you been? All hell is breaking loose." Officer Olander intercepted Adam as he approached. "The mayor and Mr. Kerrigan are in your office."

"Did they say why?" Adam grabbed the envelope Olander held out to him.

"They didn't say, but it doesn't look like a social call."

"All right. I'd better see what the two gentlemen want."

He set his hat on the rack, noticing Joshua Kerrigan held an envelope in his hand. His stomach lurched even as his face remained impassive.

"Mayor, Mr. Kerrigan. What can I do for you?" He took a seat at his desk, motioning to the other chairs. Both men remained standing.

Kerrigan tossed the envelope in front of Adam. "I received these this morning, along with the note."

Adam looked inside, knowing what he'd see. He read the note then glanced up at the men. "Have both of you seen these?"

They nodded. Mayor Timmons lowered himself into a chair while Julia's father remained standing.

"I was at Julia's last night when someone dropped off the same photos—without the note."

"You were with her? Why?" Kerrigan asked.

"She told me about being harassed and having her garage broken in to. She'd also received a couple of these photos via email. I'd been checking out what happened and made arrangements for a security firm to install an alarm system." He pinned Kerrigan with a stare. "You should know Julia and I are working to get back together."

Joshua glared back at Adam before sinking into a chair. He'd hoped Adam's return might trigger a reconciliation. It never occurred to him it might be this soon. "And the photos?"

"They were taken during our senior year in high school. I suppose there was no reason for him to make them public before now."

"Someone's been obsessed with her since high school," Timmons murmured, shaking his head slowly. "Whoever it is doesn't want the two of you back together. What of the note?"

Adam drew in a breath. "As far as what it

implies, it was true at the time. I was eighteen. Julia didn't turn eighteen until the following summer. The statute of limitations is five years, so no charges can be filed at his point."

"We'd never file anyway," Kerrigan said, beginning to direct his anger away from Adam. "It appears he's out to damage your reputation enough for you to quit and leave town. You won't let that happen, correct?"

"No sir, not unless the council asks for my resignation. Even if I'm no longer police chief, I'll stay." He leaned forward to emphasize his words. "I'll not leave Julia again."

The room fell silent as each considered the options.

"Right now my efforts must be directed toward identifying the perpetrator and getting him off the streets. I've got a computer and cyber expert, Vic Nader, coming in from Spokane this morning. He's going to go through Julia's computer, see if he can trace anything." Adam looked at Olander as the officer poked his head into the office.

"Got a guy named Vic here to see you, Chief."

"Good timing. Send him in."

******

"Holy crap..." Caly swore as she stared at the screen, not recognizing the images of the two

115

people. She glanced up, noticing her sister standing in her doorway. "You've got to see what someone sent me."

Julia dashed around the desk to see full screen images of her and Adam, their faces somewhat obscured.

"Oh no." She covered her mouth, tears welling in her eyes as her body began to tremble.

"Do you know them?" Caly grasped Julia's arm, concerned at her reaction.

"It's Adam and I when we were in high school. Where did you get them?"

"My God, Julia. I'm so sorry. I just opened the email and this came up."

Julia peered at the sender information. "It's from one of the main email providers. Do you recognize the name?" She shot a look at Caly.

"No. Usually these emails are from people requesting information about housing in the area. That's the only reason I opened it. It could be from anybody."

"I've got to call Adam." She grabbed her phone, punching Adam's number. "It's Julia. Caly just received an email with the photos attached. It came from a different email than the others."

"Yeah, I'm not surprised. Vic got here about an hour ago and is trying to locate the source. The sender used some type of email proxy account, but it wasn't effective. He says the guy is real sloppy and not a techie." He paced a few feet away from Vic. "How are you doing?"

"As you'd expect, knowing the guy is starting to send the pictures around." She looked up to see her father outside Caly's office. "My father just showed up. I'd better—"

"Someone sent him the photos, Julia. He already knows."

She turned her back to the door, burning with embarrassment, not wanting to face her father. "How do you know that?"

"He was at my office when I arrived, along with the mayor. I explained you've already seen them. He also knows we're trying to work things out between us. I think he'll be all right."

"I don't know what to say to him," she said as pain filled her voice.

"Remember, none of this is your fault and what we did wasn't wrong. I'll be there in an hour. I love you, Julia."

"I love you, too." She hung up and swung around to face the one man she admired above all others. The pain on his face reflected her own. He opened his arms and she flew into them, tears streaming down her face.

He tightened his arms around her. "We'll get this S.O.B, sweetheart. You can count on it."

Chapter Eleven

"Got it," Vic murmured as he focused in on the results of his work. "Here's what you need, Adam." He pointed to information on the screen before printing it. "You'll need to get a court order so the service provider will release any identifying information."

"I'll take care of it. Olander! Get in here," he called over his shoulder.

"Yes, Chief."

"This is what I need." He handed Olander notes he'd prepared while Vic did his work.

"Students, faculty, and administration employees who were at the high school between these dates. Okay," Olander said. "Anything else?"

"Once you have the list, identify anyone who is still in the area...anywhere around the lake and within fifty miles in all directions."

"That'll take time. Is it all right if I grab another officer to help me on some of it?"

"Choose one of the two who already know the situation."

"Yes, sir."

"And I need all of it by tomorrow."

Olander sucked in a breath. "We'll have it for

you.”

“A table in the back, please.” Adam slipped Julia’s hand through his arm, ignoring the stares of the diners already in the restaurant.

“They’re watching us,” Julia said, trying to shield herself behind him.

He bent down to whisper in her ear. “You’re the most beautiful woman in town. Of course they’ll stare.”

They took seats in a private corner with a good view of the front.

“Have you been able to find out anything?” Julia asked, fidgeting with the napkin in her lap while watching the other customers cast concealed looks their way.

Adam slipped an arm around her and pulled her close. “Vic identified the service provider for each email address, and a subpoena is being served for the release of identifying information. If nothing else, it should provide us with the address of where the emails originated. We already know they were sent from somewhere in Peregrine Bay. I have officers compiling information that should help lead to the person responsible. Trust me...we will get the person.” He kissed her forehead, leaving his arm around her. “How did it go with your father?”

Her mouth tilted into a grim smile. "He said the same things you have." She looked up at him. "You've both been wonderful."

A somber chuckle escaped his lips. "That's because we both love you."

They finished their lunch in silence before Adam confronted the issue yet to be addressed. He grasped her hand and squeezed it.

"A lot has happened since I came back to town. And last night, well…it was more than I expected. As much as I want to be with you, every night, I don't want you to feel pressured. You shouldn't be alone, but I don't have to be the one with you."

She blinked, unsure of what he was trying to tell her. "You don't want to stay? Have you changed your mind about us?"

He turned her to face him. "Never. I'll stay if you're sure that's what you want." He kissed her, not caring who saw.

She eased away from him, color washing her cheeks. "Yes, that's what I want."

"What the hell is going on here?"

Julia cringed when she saw who stood at their table. She squeezed Adam's thigh and sat up, leaning forward, hoping to avoid a confrontation.

"Hello, Mark. I didn't see you when we walked in."

"What are you doing here, Julia, with him?" His face reddened as he nodded toward Adam, otherwise ignoring him.

"Having lunch, of course."

"That's not what I'm talking about and you damn well know it."

Adam stood and stepped away from the table, keeping his voice low and calm. "That's enough, Walters. Julia and I are having lunch, and as you can see, we *are* together. I hope you understand my meaning without further explanation. If you want to speak with Julia about it in private, I suggest you call her for a meeting. This isn't the place."

A muscle flicked in Mark's jaw as his face blanched and eyebrows drew together. "Is this what you want, Julia?"

"Yes, it is. We can talk if you'd like, but not here. And, it won't change my mind."

******

Selena waited in Julia's office for her to return from lunch. She'd left a voice message and sent a text to Julia's phone without receiving a reply. It wouldn't have bothered her except for the email and images she received.

"Hey." Julia sounded tired as she walked to her desk. "What's going on?"

"I wanted to ask you the same thing. I...uh, got an email—"

"Oh God," Julia muttered, slumping into her

chair.

"You already know about them?"

Julia nodded, rubbing her eyes with the palms of her hands. "I've received them by email, plus someone dropped off several at home last night. Like you, Caly got them on email, but father got the full set in all their glossy glory this morning," she said, sarcasm lacing her words. She looked up, her eyes red. "Now you. I don't know who else has seen them."

"I heard father stopped by today to see you. Now I know why. How did he handle it?"

"He's angry, but not at either Adam or me."

"Have you spoken with Adam?" Selena asked, walking around Julia's desk and placing a hand on her shoulder.

"He's quite involved in finding out who's doing this. We were together last night when the photos arrived. I won't go into details, but we're trying to get back together." She exhaled a deep breath. "He spent the night."

Selena took a step back, her eyes lighting up. "That's wonderful news."

"It seems so fast." She glanced up, her eyes fused with a mix of anxiety and hope.

"Fast, are you joking? The two of you never should have split up. In my opinion it's taken almost ten years too long." Selena leaned against the desk, resting her hands on either side of her. "You may not be able to see it, but the way he looks at you sends chills through me. And in a good way. He's clearly still in love with you. What about you, do you still love him?"

Julia glanced out the window, for the first time noticing the bright sun and clear skies. "I thought I'd dealt with my feelings for him long ago. Not until he came back did I realize how much I still loved him. It's as if he's come home to me after a long journey, except we've both grown up along the way. We're different people, yet still the same. I guess I'm afraid of how strong my feelings are for him."

"Oh, Julia. From what I can tell, you have nothing to fear. And if I'm not mistaken, I believe he came back here for you more than the job."

Julia chuckled softly. "That's what he told me."

"And the rest of what's going on?"

"Adam is doing all he can to identify the person. It will take time. I just hope no more of those pictures are sent out...they're so humiliating."

"You have nothing to be embarrassed about and don't believe for a moment it will change anything with the family or the company. We'll all be together on this, as we always are."

Julia stood, giving Selena a hug. "Thank you," she breathed out, then stepped away, looking over the items on her desk. "I never realized how different it would be to work without a computer for longer than a few hours."

"Feel lost?"

"A little."

"Then maybe it's time you go home, or better yet, come with me and I'll show you Adam's new place. All he has to do is sign the final papers and it's his. I left a message a couple of hours ago and am pretty certain he'll want to finish it up today. My guess is you'll be spending a considerable amount of time there. Hold on a minute." Selena pulled her phone from her pocket. "Hi, Adam. Yes, it's all yours. How about we meet to sign the documents? Sounds good. I'll see you then. What? I'm in her office now." She held out the phone. "He wants to speak with you."

"Congratulations. It looks like you're now a homeowner." She shot a tired smile at Selena. "She mentioned taking me by it. Sure, that's fine. I'll wait for you." She handed the phone back. "He'll pick me up after signing the papers. He wants to show it to me himself."

"I don't believe the seller will mind if I give Adam the keys early." She turned to leave then stopped. "I'll need to tell him about the photos on my computer."

"He already has Caly's computer. He'll probably want yours as well."

"No problem. I'll take it with me to the signing. With luck he won't need it long."

Julia sat down as Selena closed the door,

wondering what she'd do with her time until Adam arrived. Everything she needed was on her computer.

"Julia?" Tricia asked as she opened the door. "Mark is here to see you, and he doesn't look too happy."

Julia blew out a breath. "Might as well get this over with," she murmured.

"Excuse me?"

"Nothing. Go ahead and send him back."

Some days were just born to be terrible.

******

Adam drove them to his new house in the truck, leaving Julia's car locked at her office. He refused to let her drive, not knowing what her stalker might do if he found her alone.

"Are you going to tell me what's bothering you, besides the obvious?" Adam reached over to wrap his hand around hers and tug her toward him.

She scooted over. Until he'd come back to town, her life seemed ordered and controlled. She'd updated her five-year plan for the business, decided to break it off with Mark, and set a resolution to meet someone she could love, maybe marry. Everything had turned around in a few short weeks, culminating in the nasty meeting with Mark.

"Mark came by the office. It's over."

"You don't sound too pleased about it. Having regrets?" Adam kept his eyes trained on the road ahead, his chest squeezing in anticipation of her response.

"None. I just hate the way it all came about—seeing us in the restaurant before I had a chance to tell him."

He relaxed, even though questions whirled in his head. "How close were the two of you?"

"Not close. He seemed to have bigger plans for us than I ever did. We'd kept it casual, so his actions in the restaurant were a surprise. I'd planned to break it off even before you got to town."

"Is there anything you need to tell me about your meeting with him? Any threats?"

"He'd never outright threaten me no matter how angry he is about my decision. It's not his style. He's more apt to make sure real estate business is directed to one of my competitors."

"I didn't think you had much competition."

"We're the largest firm, although several smaller companies do quite well. Most have one or two people and specialize in either sales or property management operations. No one else handles both on a large scale. We'll keep doing our jobs no matter the fallout." She leaned her head against the seat, letting out a sigh as her eyes shifted toward Adam. "Aren't you tired?"

"Exhausted. You wore me out last night." He

turned onto a side street then pulled to a stop in front of his new home.

He pushed open the front door and stood aside, sweeping his hand toward the living room. "Here it is."

Julia looked around, knowing from talking to Selena the work Adam would have to put into it. The front room and kitchen were disasters even though she could see beyond the filth to the potential.

"It needs a lot of work. I'll hire out some of it, but plan to do quite a bit myself."

"Let me know if you need help. You may not know it, but I've done a lot of home renovations, then resold them. I love the challenge."

Adam grinned as he headed down the hall. He opened the door to the master bedroom then stopped, muttering an oath.

"What is it?"

Julia walked up beside him, peering around his shoulder, noting holes smashed through the drywall, broken glass from the shattered sliding door, electrical sockets ripped from the walls, carpet soaked through with water, and the bathroom door ripped from the hinges.

"Was it like this the last time you saw it?"

"No. Stay here." He grabbed his phone, taking pictures as he surveyed the damage.

"Adam, you need to see this," Julia called from down the hall.

He took a few more shots then found her in another bedroom, also vandalized.

"The third bedroom is the same," she said, coming back to stand next to him. "So all of this happened after you and Selena walked through the last time."

"That's right."

Like the master bedroom, windows had been broken, holes smashed through walls, floors flooded with water, and ceiling lights ripped down. He continued to take pictures, walking from room to room, until he reached the guest bathroom where shower doors were broken and the toilet lay on its side, ripped from the floor and tossed in a corner. Water soaked through the vinyl floor, seeping into the wooden floors in the hallway.

"Why would anyone do this? They couldn't know you'd purchased it—not so soon."

"Shit." Adam grabbed her hand, moving in long strides to the living room then outside.

"What?"

"Your house."

Adam sped to Julia's place, hoping his instincts were wrong. She sat beside him, silent, one hand gripped in his. He pulled into her drive, noting all looked well from the outside. She ran to the front door, coming to an abrupt stop when she saw it standing open.

"Let me go in ahead of you, Julia." He doubted

anyone would still be around, but pulled out his service revolver as he pushed the door fully open, his heart sinking at the damaged furniture, broken glass, and what appeared to be paint thrown on walls. "Don't follow me yet. I'll let you know when it's all right to come in."

He moved through each room, finding nothing except more damage. This was so much worse than his place, where he'd already expected to gut most of the inside. Julia's home had been perfect. He glanced at the bed where they'd made love the night before, shaking his head at the shredded linens and mattress with long slits on each side. Broken picture frames and torn photos lay strewn across the floor. Adam knew from his experience as a detective this type of damage pointed to rage as opposed to destruction as a warning. The same person who'd sent the photos had entered both their homes, ratcheting up his anger to a dangerous level.

"My God."

Adam turned around to see Julia standing in the doorway, her hand covering her mouth as she took in the sight. He holstered his gun, wrapping his arms around her.

"It's the same person, isn't it?" Her voice shook as she worked to contain her outrage.

"I believe so, yes."

She pushed away, crossing her arms to control her anger as she walked around the room. "I want his guy, Adam. Whoever this monster is, I want to find him and make him pay."

130

Chapter Twelve

"It's not much," Adam said as they entered his studio apartment. At least he'd made his bed and thrown the dirty clothes into a pile in the corner.

She grabbed his hand, a thin smile playing on her face. "Hey, it's a lot better than my place."

He nodded, not thinking it much of an improvement. "I'll get your stuff." He'd given her a choice—his place or her father's. There'd been no hesitation when she wrapped her arms around his waist, placing a kiss on his lips. He smiled as he retrieved her suitcase from his truck.

Julia salvaged enough clothes to avoid making an emergency run to the local department store. Now all they had to decide was where to order take-out.

"Monroe," he answered his phone as he set down her suitcase. "Yes, sir. Olander and another officer were at Julia's house and mine. They'll have a complete report by morning, but I don't expect to find anything useful, such as prints. Yes, sir." Adam glanced at her as he set the phone aside.

"The mayor?"

"He heard about the break-ins. If Deke, the security technician, hadn't been called away for some emergency, your system would've been installed today and this might not have happened."

"It's not Deke's fault, Adam. I believe whoever is doing this would've found a way to get to me, even if it wasn't destroying my home. We can't change what he did." She stepped next to him, letting her hand move up to his shoulder, then his neck, feeling the tension in his muscles.

"No, but we can find the S.O.B. and put him in jail." He let his head drop forward, allowing her fingers work their magic on his neck and upper back.

"Take off your shirt and sit down. You're as tight as a drum."

He removed his shirt and lowered himself onto the bed as she climbed behind him, using her thumbs to push deep into his tissues, enjoying the sound of his groan. She felt the tissues relax and let her hands move to a kneading motion, her palms pressing into his shoulders and upper back.

"Where did you learn to do this?"

"I took a class while in school. One of those extension courses."

"Who did you practice on?" he asked, his voice lowering, becoming hoarse.

"Anyone who'd let me."

She could hear a difference in his voice, the stress giving way to a tranquil peace.

"Okay, lie on your stomach."

He didn't say a word, just did as Julia instructed, stretching out on the mattress, feeling her move behind him. She started at his shoulders, continuing to knead and massage, working her way down in long, sure strokes. Her fingers caressed his skin at times, then pushed deeper to relax tense muscles. His eyelids grew heavy and yet his body felt sensitized, fully in tune with her touch.

Julia moved lower, kneading his lower back, hearing his breathing slow until certain he'd fallen asleep. She drew a leg over him, rolling off the bed when a hand snaked out to grab her wrist.

"Where do you think you're going?" he asked, pulling her back to him, wrapping his arms around her.

She sighed as his lips swept kisses along her neck, across her jaw, until he'd captured her mouth. The kiss was slow, his tongue sending shivers of desire through her. He increased the pressure, his mouth becoming insistent, claiming hers with a deep hunger, setting her body on fire.

Her hands moved up his back to his neck, her motions becoming almost frantic as she shredded fingers through his hair, holding him to her. The heat in her body increased, creating an aching need for more.

He broke the kiss, moving his lips down her neck to the hollow at the base of her throat.

"Adam," she breathed out, pushing into him,

trying to get closer. "I want...I..."

He chuckled softly. "I know baby. I know." His hand moved to the top of her blouse, releasing one button then another, before releasing the front clasp of her bra and pushing the fabric aside, letting his gaze wander over her. "You are so beautiful," he whispered, as he continued his slow ministrations, not stopping until they both found release before drifting off to sleep.

******

"We just received the information, Chief." Olander handed Adam the transmission from the Internet service provider, showing an address.

Adam scanned the document. "Do you know this address?"

"It's the library."

Adam grabbed his hat and started for the door. "You coming?" he asked Olander when he noticed the officer hadn't moved.

"Yes, sir."

"Then get moving."

They didn't need a car. The library stood a block away from the police station on a quiet street, lined on both sides by evergreens. Built in the fifties, it stood three stories high plus a basement. Adam remembered exploring the basement with Julia, finding all kinds of treasures before the head librarian found them and booted them outside. They'd been banned for a month. He wondered if she was still around.

"May I help you?" A young man stepped up to the information counter, his eyes glancing at Adam's badge.

"I'm Police Chief Monroe. Is the head librarian in?"

"I'd be happy to help you, Chief Monroe." A woman walked up next to Adam. "She isn't here right now, but I'm her assistant, Mrs. Johannsen."

"Nice meeting you. This is Officer Olander."

She smiled at the man and nodded. "How can I assist you?"

"May we talk privately?"

"Of course. Follow me."

It didn't take Adam long to explain the situation, omitting names and specifics about what had been sent.

"The computers we offer for library use don't allow users to access the Internet, except for partner sites such as other libraries. I don't see how anyone could establish and use an email account from here."

"What about employee computers?"

"Yes, they do have access, but I can't imagine any of them being involved. Most have been here for a long time."

"May I see a list of employees, including when

they were hired?" Adam asked.

Mrs. Johannsen let out a sigh, opened a computer program and generated a list. "Here you are."

He scanned it, noting just two men, both in their sixties. "You're absolutely certain there is no other computer a patron could use that might have full access?"

Her eyes widened, brows rising. "Well, there is one old machine that does get used on occasion by people needing to do a little more research while they're here. We offer it on a limited basis and only to locals we know."

"May we see it?"

They followed her to an office behind hers which held a few bookcases and a desk, upon which sat an old computer.

"Let me turn it on. I don't believe it's been used since yesterday."

"Do you keep a log of who has access?"

She shook her head. "Really, there are perhaps six or seven people who use it, and that's spread out. Most are older people without a computer at home plus a couple others." She turned as the young man poked his head into the office.

"Excuse me, Mrs. Johannsen, but Mr. Farrell is asking if he may use the computer."

Adam's head jerked at the science teacher's name.

"Please tell him I'll be out in a few minutes."

"Yes, ma'am."

Mrs. Johannsen turned back toward the men. "It's ready now if you want to check it."

"What I'll need to do is take it back to the station so our computer expert may check it. But, I would like to ask about Mr. Farrell. Does he use this computer often?"

"He's probably the most frequent user, maybe once or twice a week. His house is quite far out of town and the Internet access at the school can be quite slow. He does research here, using this for additional searches when he can't find what he wants in books."

"Besides today, when was the last time you saw him?"

"Let me think. Maybe last Friday."

"Olander, shut down the computer. We'll need the whole set up back at the station so Vic can check it out." He shifted his attention to the librarian. "I'd like to speak with Mr. Farrell for a moment. May I use your office?"

He followed her to the front, spotting Mr. Farrell speaking to another gentlemen.

"Mr. Farrell?"

"Ah, Adam Monroe. That's twice in just a few days. How are you?"

"Good. May I have a word with you, in private?" Adam asked, noting the other gentleman excused himself.

Farrell eyed him, not at all certain he wanted any further discussions with the police chief. "I have little time today, but I could set up a time to talk. Perhaps tomorrow?"

"Today, Mr. Farrell. Now. We can talk here or go to the station, whichever works better for you."

"All right, if it must be now. Let's get it over with."

Adam closed the door behind them, indicating a chair to Farrell and taking Mrs. Johannsen's chair for himself. He watched as Farrell crossed one leg over the other, then switched legs as his gaze wandered everywhere except toward Adam. He let the man stew for a minute before starting.

Finally, Farrell broke the silence. "What did you need to speak with me about?"

"What do you use the library's private computer for? The one in the back room."

Farrell's brows knitted together in confusion. "The computer? Research on various science topics."

"You can't use any others?"

"Access at the school is inordinately slow. It takes four or five times as long to find what I need than when I come here."

"And at home?"

"I live almost fifteen miles from town. Since I do a great deal of fact checking here at the library it makes sense to use their computer. It's free and Mrs. Johannsen is quite gracious in letting me use it. What is this about?"

"Have you ever used this computer to establish an email account, send messages?"

"Never," he huffed. "Why would I do such a thing?" Farrell fidgeted, uncrossing his legs and crossing his arms.

"You've never set up an email account, using it to send harassing emails?" Adam kept his voice calm, his body relaxed, watching Farrell's agitation grow.

"I believe this conversation is over." Farrell started to stand.

"Sit down, Mr. Farrell. I found you outside Ms. Kerrigan's home the night a set of explicit photographs were left at her door. You had no witnesses to confirm your reason for being there, but I let you leave. Now we've established that the library computer you've had access to has been used to set up bogus email accounts. Accounts used to send harassing emails and photos to Ms. Kerrigan and others." At least that's what Adam hoped Vic would determine.

"That's horrible, but I can assure you it's not me." His already agitated voice raised an octave as he spoke.

"You've known Julia Kerrigan since she took your classes in high school. You would have been twenty-seven or eight at the time, and found yourself attracted to a beautiful student ten years your junior. You couldn't have her but you fixated on her, didn't you?"

"No. Absolutely not."

"And you followed her. Took pictures of her with someone else. Pictures that are now being used to harass her and those she loves."

"Never! I'd never do anything like that. Besides, I'm not..." Farrell clamped his mouth shut and sat back in his chair.

"Besides, you're not...what?" Adam leaned forward, placing his arms on the desk.

Farrell raised a hand, wiping away the moisture forming on his forehead. "Nothing."

"What aren't you, Mr. Farrell?"

He shook his head, not wanting to discuss it any further.

"All right. I guess we can finish this discussion at the station."

"No. Wait." Farrell clasped his hands in his lap, his eyes darting around the room before his gaze focused on Adam. "I'm not attracted to women. I'm gay. Have been since high school."

A burst of air escaped Adam's lips at the announcement. He hadn't seen this coming.

"Do you have anyone who can confirm where you were yesterday?"

"The school can verify I was on campus most of

the day. I came here for a short time yesterday, as Mrs. Johannsen will confirm, then went home.”

“Can anyone verify you were at home, all night?”

“Yes. My partner and I were together from about five o’clock until I left this morning. I never left the house.”

“I’ll need your partner’s name and a way to contact him.” He waited while Farrell wrote down a name and phone number. “Thank you, Mr. Farrell. I appreciate your cooperation and hope you will understand the need to keep this meeting confidential—for Ms. Kerrigan’s sake. I’ll be back in touch if I have more questions.”

Chapter Thirteen

Adam's mind raced through other possibilities. Before leaving the library, he'd obtained a list of everyone who accessed the computer with approximate dates over the last two weeks. Olander had already begun matching it to the list of people still living in the area when Julia and he attended high school.

He grabbed his phone on the first ring. "Monroe."

"Hey." Julia's voice triggered a mix of anticipation and warmth to flow through him. "I have some news. The insurance investigator did his inspection this morning. Apparently I have coverage for a rental unit while my house is being repaired."

"All right..." He'd hoped she would stay with him, but knew his studio would feel cramped within a few days.

"It's a set amount per day, but I'd be able to rent a two bedroom with it. He estimates the repair work at two to three months, but will wait for the contractor's report. What do you say?"

"Are you asking me to move in with you?" He smiled, hoping he'd read her right.

"Well...yes. I just thought...I guess I'm not

certain what I thought. You can certainly keep your place."

"Sounds good, sweetheart. When can I move my stuff?"

He could hear her let out a breath. "Tonight after work."

"That quick, huh?"

"It pays to know people," she joked. "Caly manages the property, so I have immediate access. It rents mainly to tourists for a week up to three months. The owner's unit is vacant and he has no plans to come out this summer. He lives in Seattle and has already given his approval."

"Where are you now?"

"At the office. Why?"

"I don't want you at your place alone. Meet me at the studio at six. I'll pack what little I have then we'll go to your house to pick up anything else you need that's salvageable."

"All right. See you at six."

"And Julia?"

"Yes?"

"I love you." He didn't wait for a response, seeing Olander coming toward his office.

"I have something you need to look at, Chief." He dropped a plastic evidence bag on Adam's desk containing what appeared to be a credit card case. "Here, you'll need these." Olander handed him a pair of gloves.

Adam slipped them on and pulled out the contents of the case, his eyes widening at the name on the cards. "Where did you find this?"

"In Ms. Kerrigan's living room, under a pile of books and cushions. I took it because of the contents, thinking Ms. Kerrigan would need it back. I didn't check the name on the cards until now."

"I'd better call Julia before we do anything further. Keep working on the list—"

"It's done." Olander handed the final cross-matched list to Adam. "He's on it."

Adam scanned the list which contained just four people—one he'd already eliminated, one lived in a retirement home, and a third was a female in her eighties. He held the card case of the last person on the list in his hand.

"All right. Let's not jump to conclusions until I've spoken with Julia and done a little more checking." He looked up at Olander. "This is between us until I get more information."

"Right."

He grabbed his phone, waiting for Julia to pick up.

"I'm heading out to a meeting. What's up?"

"Is there any chance Mark may have left his credit card case in the living room at your house?"

"None. He came to my house once to pick up a sign for an event. I don't believe he even came inside."

"How long ago was that?" Adam slid the case back in the evidence bag, tossing the gloves in the trash.

"Maybe a month ago, but I can check my calendar."

"No need right now. As long as you're certain he would not have left it in your house."

"Absolutely. Why?"

"Olander found it during his investigation of the vandalism. He thought it was yours until he went through it today."

"Mark? You think he's the one doing all this?" Disbelief and shock laced her words. "But why?"

"I won't know any more until I speak with him."

"He'll be at the meeting I'm going to. What shall I do?" Julia felt the blood drain from her face at the realization the man she'd been dating might be capable of the actions against her and Adam.

"It's important you act normal, as if you know nothing of his possible connection. He may be able to explain it all. Where's the meeting?"

"City Hall."

"I'll be waiting for him when the meeting ends."

******

Julia's hands felt clammy by the time Mark entered the room. All chairs except for one across from her were taken. She'd hoped he'd sit where he couldn't watch her, gauge her reactions to the many questions running through her mind about the emails, photos, and destruction. Her brain couldn't stop asking why he'd jeopardize everything in an attempt to humiliate and discredit her.

"I heard about your house, Julia. Do they have any idea who did it?"

Mark's question jerked her gaze toward him. Something in his eyes caught her attention, warning her to say little.

"Not yet."

"For what it's worth, I'm sorry."

She nodded, feeling her skin crawl, not believing he felt an ounce of remorse for the damage.

"Shall we start the meeting?" The Downtown Business Alliance committee chair passed out folders, then began discussing open actions for the Fourth of July celebrations.

Julia found it hard to keep focused as the meeting progressed, glad she held a minor role in the celebration. Each time she glanced up, Mark's eyes were on her. She squirmed, wondering if he had any idea who would be waiting for him after the meeting.

******

"I'll take Olander with me." Adam finished

briefing Mayor Timmons on what they'd found and who they suspected of the crimes.

"I still can't believe Mark would do such things. Other than college, he's been in town his entire life, getting involved in civic issues, as well as being a positive force on the City Council. His father retired a few years ago, lives not far from my place."

"He hasn't been proven guilty yet, but everything points to him. The truth is, it makes sense given his interest in Julia. He didn't have a chance with her in high school and they attended different colleges. It appears he bided his time once he returned home, perhaps not feeling the rush since I wasn't around. He finally got his chance with her, then I returned. I've worked similar cases in Washington and it still makes no sense how an otherwise sane person would snap to this degree."

"If what you're saying is true, he's been stalking her since high school, or at least obsessed with her. It's a dangerous emotion. Do you want me with you?" Timmons asked.

"No. Olander and I will handle this, although you might be prepared for backlash. I'm sure there will be a lot of people who'll defend Walters. We'll take him to the station for questions. I'll get in touch with you as soon as I know more."

******

"Looks like we have the event ready to go. Thanks to all of you for the hard work." The committee chair ended the meeting, picking up her files as people left the room.

Julia continued to sit, waiting until Mark left the room, although he seemed to be in no hurry. She wanted to see his reaction when Adam explained why he was waiting. Sensing Mark staring at her from across the table, Julia looked up.

"Do you need help cleaning up your house?" he asked.

"No. I've hired someone to handle it." She rose, slinging her purse on her shoulder, taking slow steps and hoping Mark would precede her out. Instead, he waited for her, opening the door to the hallway.

"Well, Chief Monroe. Have you come to meet Julia?" Mark smirked.

"No. I've come to speak with you. I'd like you to accompany Officer Olander and me to the station. We have quite a few questions for you."

Mark glanced at his watch. "Unfortunately, I'm already late for a meeting. Another time."

"No, today, Mr. Walters."

Mark's gaze shifted between Adam, Olander, Julia, and the other people who'd congregated in the hall. His hands began to shake as beads of sweat formed on his brow.

Adam hoped he wouldn't run. He wanted Mark

all in one piece for the questioning, but he'd take him in any way he could get him.

Without warning, Mark dropped his notebook and darted toward the stairs behind him.

"Walters, stop!" Adam ran after him. "Go out the front," he called over his shoulder to Olander as he followed Mark down the stairs. At least he'd had the good sense to post additional officers outside each exit. Walters would never be able to get by all of them.

Adam pushed through the back exit to see Mark swinging at an officer before being shoved up against a wall, hands behind him as the officer frisked him.

"He's clean, Chief."

"Cuff him, transport him to the station, and book him on charges of resisting arrest."

******

Adam drove the dark winding road to Selena's house, where she and Calypso sat with Julia, keeping her occupied until he arrived. It had been a long interrogation, Mark not giving up anything, talking in circles, then breaking down, but not confessing.

A search warrant of his home yielded a desktop computer, laptop, additional cell phone, and several notebooks. Vic had decided to take some extra time in Peregrine Bay as a vacation. Now he'd make some extra cash.

Mark would be arraigned in a few days, probably post bail—assuming the judge allowed it—then they'd go from there. He'd given up enough information for them to know they had the right person. Adam felt certain they'd get a conviction.

"Hey, Adam. Come on in. Julia's in the kitchen with Caly."

He strode straight to Julia, taking her into his arms, and stroking her back.

"Is it over?"

"Yes. He lawyered up and didn't confess, but we have all we need to get him convicted. You ready to go?"

She nodded, taking his hand, looking toward her sisters. "I'll be staying with Adam."

Selena and Caly watched them leave.

"Care to bet on how long it is before the wedding?" Caly asked.

Selena chuckled. "Six months, tops."

"Darn. That's what I would've guessed. I'll go with five."

They shook hands as Adam's taillights disappeared into the distance.

Epilogue

They were both wrong. Three months later, half the town celebrated in Joshua Kerrigan's large back yard.

It hadn't taken Adam long to ask her to marry him and about two seconds for Julia to agree. They'd thought of going to Vegas, until her stepmother, Joannie, and father, rejected the idea before it had a chance to bloom. Joannie swore she, Selena, and Calypso could pull it off in time for an August wedding. Now, over three hundred guests enjoyed music, food, and the spectacular lake view after witnessing the beautiful ceremony.

Adam and Julia also accomplished much in the three months. The contractor finished Julia's house two weeks before the wedding, then finished Adam's hours before his bachelor party. They'd made the decision to rent her house and move into his as soon as returning from their honeymoon, moving her furniture into his place.

"I didn't think the weeks would ever pass." Adam wrapped an arm around Julia's waist, drawing her close.

She laughed. "Between Joannie and the contractor, it seemed we never had a free minute when we didn't have to make a decision. It amazes me how we juggled so much with all of us focused on this." She nodded toward the yard, overflowing with guests.

"At least we'll get some time alone on our honeymoon."

"You aren't worried about leaving the department so soon after you started as the chief?" She snuggled next to him, waving to friends standing near the water's edge.

"It's been almost six months, and no, I'm not concerned. They're professionals, plus they know how to reach me. It's not like we'll be out of communication."

"I wish we were." She leaned up for a kiss, seeing her father come up behind Adam, and turned to give him a hug.

"You all did a splendid job. Now that it's over, I might be able to spend some time with my wife." Joshua chuckled, thinking of the chaos a wedding created, and his wife had been in the center of it.

"If you two will excuse me, I'm going to visit with my sisters." Julia accepted another flute of champagne on her way down the steps to the yard, joining Selena, Calypso, Danielle, and Lily at a table under a large pine.

"Quite a family you have, Mr. Kerrigan." Adam nodded toward the women, a look of affection spreading across his face.

"I think it's time you call me Joshua, don't you?"

Adam tilted his glass toward his father-in-law. "Guess you're right."

"Did your parents ever mention Joannie and I have had dinner with them a few times over the past year?" Joshua asked.

"No. They never said a word."

"How do you think I learned about your desire to return to Peregrine Bay?"

Adam's eyes widened in surprise. "It was you who threw my name in the hat?"

Joshua's face remained impassive, although his mouth tilted up slightly at the corners.

"Even after what happened with Julia?"

"Especially after that. The two of you were always meant for each other. It didn't take a genius to see what needed to happen." Joshua brought the glass to his mouth, taking a sip of the twenty-five-year old single malt scotch. "Ah, that is good."

Adam watched Julia laughing with her sisters as he listened. "Thank you. I'd been looking for a way to get back here for a long time."

"I knew the previous chief would be retiring and the timing seemed right. Your skills would've been wasted as an officer, but as the chief, well...that made sense."

"I owe you one, Joshua."

"You owe me nothing except to make my

daughter happy. And give me grandchildren."

******

"So, who's next?" Danielle took a sip of wine while glancing between Selena and Caly.

"It's not going to be me, so Selena, the task it up to you." Calypso had no plans to marry, at least for many years and maybe never. She just didn't seem to have the genes needed to give up her carefree life for one man and children.

The others looked at Selena, waiting for her reaction. Of the five, she was the most reserved, shy by nature, rarely drank, and dated maybe three or four times a year. She'd never had a serious relationship as far as they knew.

"Well, guess it's time I go for another soft drink." She started to rise.

"Oh no you don't," Caly cut in. "When was the last time you went on a date, or even to a party?"

"I'm here today, aren't I?" Selena shot back, becoming somewhat agitated.

"Julia's wedding reception doesn't count. When was the last time you went to a party that didn't include family?" Caly raised her hand to the server, grabbing another glass of wine.

Selena couldn't remember when she last attended a party not affiliated with family or work. It just wasn't her thing, but maybe it should be.

Unlike Caly, Selena knew she wanted to meet someone, fall in love and marry, but she sure hadn't met anyone going about it her way.

"I don't recall the last time." She glanced at the crowd, noting a circle of men standing near the bar, wondering if she should just go up and introduce herself, knowing she never would.

"Here's the deal." Caly leaned forward, setting her glass on the table. "There's a party at the north end of the lake next weekend. It's an open party held by a prominent businessman, celebrating the end of summer. You're coming with me."

Danielle and Lily watched the interplay, eyes wide. The twins had never witnessed this type of interaction between their older sisters and were fascinated by it.

"Oh no I'm not. There isn't a chance I'll go to a party without an invitation."

"Caly may be right, Selena. Perhaps going to a party with people outside our hometown might be good for you. You might feel more relaxed and you'll certainly meet men you wouldn't find here." Julia tipped back her head, finishing the last drop of champagne and setting the glass on the table.

"You're siding with her?" Selena couldn't believe Julia's words of encouragement.

"I'm siding with you. You work, go to the gym, work some more, then go to bed. The next day the routine starts all over again."

"You make me sound dull, without a life."

"Exactly!" Caly chimed in. "It's settled. We'll go to the party next weekend. Unless you're too much of a coward."

Selena gritted her teeth at being called both boring and a coward in the span of less than a minute.

"Fine. I'll go and before I leave I'll have a great time with a gorgeous guy. Satisfied?" Selena's voice rang with determination.

"Oh yeah. Quite satisfied." Caly held her glass in the air. "Here's to Selena's big adventure," she said, laughing as the others joined the toast.

Selena slumped back in her chair, wondering what in the world she'd gotten herself into.

Join me in the continuation of the Peregrine Bay series with the story of Selena and Linc in book two, Our Kind of Love, due to release in 2015

Thank you for taking the time to read Reclaiming Love. If you enjoyed it, please consider telling your friends or posting a short review. Word of mouth is an author's best friend and much appreciated.

Please join my reader's group to be notified of my New Releases at:
http://www.shirleendavies.com/contact-me.html

I care about quality, so if you find something in error, please contact me via email at
shirleen@shirleendavies.com

About the Author

Shirleen Davies writes romance—historical, contemporary, and romantic suspense. She grew up in Southern California, attended Oregon State University, and has degrees from San Diego State University and the University of Maryland. During the day she provides consulting services to small and mid-sized businesses. But her real passion is writing emotionally charged stories of flawed people who find redemption through love and acceptance. She now lives with her husband in a beautiful town in northern Arizona.

Shirleen loves to hear from her readers.

Write to her at: shirleen@shirleendavies.com
Visit her website: http://www.shirleendavies.com
Sign up to be notified of New Releases:
http://www.shirleendavies.com/contact-me.html
Comment on her blog:
http://www.shirleendavies.com/blog.html
Facebook Fan Page:
https://www.facebook.com/ShirleenDaviesAuthor
Twitter:
http://twitter.com/shirleendavies

Google+:

http://www.gplusid.com/shirleendavies

LinkedIn:

http://www.linkedin.com/in/shirleendaviesauthor

Pinterest:

http://www.pinterest.com/shirleendavies

Tsu:

http://www.tsu.co/shirleendavies

Other Books by Shirleen Davies

Tougher than the Rest – Book One
MacLarens of Fire Mountain Historical Western Romance Series
"A passionate, fast-paced story set in the untamed western frontier by an exciting new voice in historical romance."

Niall MacLaren is the oldest of four brothers, and the undisputed leader of the family. A widower, and single father, his focus is on building the MacLaren ranch into the largest and most successful in northern Arizona. He is serious about two things—his responsibility to the family and his future marriage to the wealthy, well-connected widow who will secure his place in the territory's destiny.

Katherine is determined to live the life she's dreamed about. With a job waiting for her in the growing town of Los Angeles, California, the young teacher from Philadelphia begins a journey across the United States with only a couple of trunks and her spinster companion. Life is perfect for this adventurous, beautiful young woman, until an accident throws her into the arms of the one man who can destroy it all.

Fighting his growing attraction and strong desire for the beautiful stranger, Niall is more determined than ever to push emotions aside to focus on his goals of wealth and political gain. But looking into the clear, blue eyes of the woman who could ruin everything, Niall discovers he will have to harden his heart and be tougher than he's ever been in his life...Tougher than the Rest.

Faster than the Rest – Book Two
MacLarens of Fire Mountain Historical Western Romance Series
"Headstrong, brash, confident, and complex, the MacLarens of Fire Mountain will captivate you with strong characters set in the wild and rugged western frontier."
Handsome, ruthless, young U.S. Marshal Jamie MacLaren had lost everything—his parents, his family connections, and his childhood sweetheart—but now he's back in Fire Mountain and ready for another chance. Just as he successfully reconnects with his family and starts to rebuild his life, he gets the unexpected and unwanted assignment of rescuing the woman who broke his heart.

Beautiful, wealthy Victoria Wicklin chose money and power over love, but is now fighting for her life—or is she? Who has she become in the seven years since she left Fire Mountain to take up her life in San Francisco? Is she really as innocent as she says?

Marshal MacLaren struggles to learn the truth and do his job, but the past and present lead him in different directions as his heart and brain wage battle. Is Victoria a victim or a villain? Is life offering him another chance, or just another heartbreak?

As Jamie and Victoria struggle to uncover past secrets and come to grips with their shared passion, another danger arises. A life-altering danger that is out of their control and threatens to destroy any chance for a shared future.

Harder than the Rest – Book Three
MacLarens of Fire Mountain Historical Western Romance Series
"They are men you want on your side. Hard, confident, and loyal, the MacLarens of Fire Mountain will seize your attention from the first page."
Will MacLaren is a hardened, plain-speaking bounty hunter. His life centers on finding men guilty of horrendous crimes and making sure justice is done. There is no place in his world for the carefree attitude he carried years before when a tragic event destroyed his dreams.

Amanda is the daughter of a successful Colorado rancher. Determined and proud, she works hard to prove she is as capable as any man and worthy to be her father's heir. When a stranger arrives, her independent nature collides with the strong pull toward the handsome ranch hand. But is he what he seems and could his secrets endanger her as well as her family?

The last thing Will needs is to feel passion for another woman. But Amanda elicits feelings he thought were long buried. Can Will's desire for her change him? Or will the vengeance he seeks against the one man he wants to destroy—a dangerous opponent without a conscious—continue to control his life?

Stronger than the Rest – Book Four
MacLarens of Fire Mountain Historical Western Romance Series
"Smart, tough, and capable, the MacLarens protect their own no matter the odds. Set against America's rugged frontier, the stories of the men from Fire Mountain are complex, fast-paced, and a must read for anyone who enjoys non-stop action and romance."

Drew MacLaren is focused and strong. He has achieved all of his goals except one—to return to the MacLaren ranch and build the best horse breeding program in the west. His successful career as an attorney is about to give way to his ranching roots when a bullet changes everything.

Tess Taylor is the quiet, serious daughter of a Colorado ranch family with dreams of her own. Her shy nature keeps her from developing friendships outside of her close-knit family until Drew enters her life. Their relationship grows. Then a bullet, meant for another, leaves him paralyzed and determined to distance himself from the one woman he's come to love.

Convinced he is no longer the man Tess needs, Drew focuses on regaining the use of his legs and recapturing a life he thought lost. But danger of another kind threatens those he cares about—including Tess—forcing him to rethink his future.

Can Drew overcome the barriers that stand between him, the safety of his friends and family, and a life with the woman he loves? To do it all, he has to be strong. Stronger than the Rest.

Deadlier than the Rest – Book Five

MacLarens of Fire Mountain Historical Western Romance Series

"A passionate, heartwarming story of the iconic MacLarens of Fire Mountain. This captivating historical western romance grabs your attention from the start with an engrossing story encompassing two romances set against the rugged backdrop of the burgeoning western frontier."

Connor MacLaren's search has already stolen eight years of his life. Now he is close to finding what he seeks—Meggie, his missing sister. His quest leads him to the growing city of Salt Lake and an encounter with the most captivating woman he has ever met.

Grace is the third wife of a Mormon farmer, forced into a life far different from what she'd have chosen. Her independent spirit longs for choices governed only by her own heart and mind. To achieve her dreams, she must hide behind secrets and half-truths, even as her heart pulls her towards the ruggedly handsome Connor.

Known as cool and uncompromising, Connor MacLaren lives by a few, firm rules that have served him well and kept him alive. However, danger stalks Connor, even to the front range of the beautiful Wasatch Mountains, threatening those he cares about and impacting his ability to find his sister.

Can Connor protect himself from those who seek his death? Will his eight-year search lead him to his sister while unlocking the secrets he knows are held tight within Grace, the woman who has captured his heart?

Read this heartening story of duty, honor, passion, and love in book five of the MacLarens of Fire Mountain series.

Wilder than the Rest – Book Six
MacLarens of Fire Mountain Historical Western Romance Series

"A captivating historical western romance set in the burgeoning and treacherous city of San Francisco. Go along for the ride in this gripping story that seizes your attention from the very first page."

"If you're a reader who wants to discover an entire family of characters you can fall in love with, this is the series for you." – Authors to Watch

Pierce is a rough man, but happy in his new life as a Special Agent. Tasked with defending the rights of the federal government, Pierce is a cunning gunslinger always ready to tackle the next job. That is, until he finds out that his new job involves Mollie Jamison.

Mollie can be a lot to handle. Headstrong and independent, Mollie has chosen a life of danger and intrigue guaranteed to prove her liquor-loving father wrong. She will make something of herself, and no one, not even arrogant Pierce MacLaren, will stand in her way.

A secret mission brings them together, but will their attraction to each other prove deadly in their hunt for justice? The payoff for success is high, much higher than any assignment either has taken before. But will the damage to their hearts and souls be too much to bear? Can Pierce and Mollie find a way to overcome their misgivings and work together as one?

Second Summer – Book One
MacLarens of Fire Mountain Contemporary Romance Series

"In this passionate Contemporary Romance, author Shirleen Davies introduces her readers to the modern day MacLarens starting with Heath MacLaren, the head of the family."
The Chairman of both the MacLaren Cattle Co. and MacLaren Land Development, Heath MacLaren is a success professionally—his personal life is another matter.

Following a divorce after a long, loveless marriage, Heath spends his time with women who are beautiful and passionate, yet unable to provide what he longs for

. . .

Heath has never experienced love even though he witnesses it every day between his younger brother, Jace, and wife, Caroline. He wants what they have, yet spends his time with women too young to understand what drives him and too focused on themselves to be true companions.

It's been two years since Annie's husband died, leaving her to build a new life. He was her soul mate and confidante. She has no desire to find a replacement, yet longs for male friendship.

Annie's closest friend in Fire Mountain, Caroline MacLaren, is determined to see Annie come out of her shell after almost two years of mourning. A chance meeting with Heath turns into an offer to be a part of the MacLaren Foundation Board and an opportunity for a life outside her home sanctuary which has also become her prison. The platonic friendship that builds between Annie and Heath points to a future where each may rely on the other without the bonds a romance would entail. *However, without consciously seeking it, each yearns for more . . .*

The MacLaren Development Company is booming with Heath at the helm. His meetings at a partner company with the young, beautiful marketing director, who makes no secret of her desire for him, are a temptation. But is she the type of woman he truly wants?

Annie's acceptance of the deep, yet passionless, friendship with Heath sustains her, lulling her to believe it is all she needs. At least until Heath drops a bombshell, forcing Annie to realize that what she took for friendship is actually a deep, lasting love. One she doesn't want to lose.

Each must decide to settle—or fight for it all.

Hard Landing – Book Two
MacLarens of Fire Mountain Contemporary Romance Series

Trey MacLaren is a confident, poised Navy pilot. He's focused, loyal, ethical, and a natural leader. He is also on his way to what he hopes will be a lasting relationship and marriage with fellow pilot, Jesse Evans.

Jesse has always been driven. Her graduation from the Naval Academy and acceptance into the pilot training program are all she thought she wanted—until she discovered love with Trey MacLaren

Trey and Jesse's lives are filled with fast flying, friends, and the demands of their military careers. Lives each has settled into with a passion. At least until the day Trey receives a letter that could change his and Jesse's lives forever.

It's been over two years since Trey has seen the woman in Pensacola. Her unexpected letter stuns him and pushes Jesse into a tailspin from which she might not pull back.

Each must make a choice. Will the choice Trey makes cause him to lose Jesse forever? Will she follow her heart or her head as she fights for a chance to save the love she's found? Will their independent decisions collide, forcing them to give up on a life together?

One More Day – Book Three
MacLarens of Fire Mountain Contemporary Romance Series

Cameron "Cam" Sinclair is smart, driven, and dedicated, with an easygoing temperament that belies his strong will and the personal ambitions he holds close. Besides his family, his job as head of IT at the MacLaren Cattle Company and his position as a Search and Rescue volunteer are all he needs to make him happy. At least that's what he thinks until he meets, and is instantly drawn to, fellow SAR volunteer, Lainey Devlin.

Lainey is compassionate, independent, and ready to break away from her manipulative and controlling fiancé. Just as her decision is made, she's called into a major search and rescue effort, where once again, her path crosses with the intriguing, and much too handsome, Cam Sinclair. But Lainey's plans are set. An opportunity to buy a flourishing preschool in northern Arizona is her chance to make a fresh start, and nothing, not even her fierce attraction to Cam Sinclair, will impede her plans.

As Lainey begins to settle into her new life, an unexpected danger arises —threats from an unknown assailant—someone who doesn't believe she belongs in Fire Mountain. The more Lainey begins to love her new home, the greater the danger becomes. Can she accept the help and protection Cam offers while ignoring her consuming desire for him?

Even if Lainey accepts her attraction to Cam, will he ever be able to come to terms with his own driving ambition and allow himself to consider a different life than the one he's always pictured? A life with the one woman who offers more than he'd ever hoped to find?

All Your Nights – Book Four
MacLarens of Fire Mountain Contemporary Romance Series
"Romance, adventure, cowboys, suspense—everything you want in a contemporary western romance novel."

Kade Taylor likes living on the edge. As an undercover agent for the DEA and a former Special Ops team member, his current assignment seems tame—keep tabs on a bookish Ph.D. candidate the agency believes is connected to a ruthless drug cartel.

Brooke Sinclair is weeks away from obtaining her goal of a doctoral degree. She spends time finalizing her presentation and relaxing with another student who seems to want nothing more than her friendship. That's fine with Brooke. Her last serious relationship ended in a broken engagement.

Her future is set, safe and peaceful, just as she's always planned—until Agent Taylor informs her she's under suspicion for illegal drug activities.

Kade and his DEA team obtain evidence which exonerates Brooke while placing her in danger from those who sought to use her. As Kade races to take down the drug cartel while protecting Brooke, he must also find common ground with the former suspect—a woman he desires with increasing intensity.

At odds with her better judgment, Brooke finds the more time she spends with Kade, the more she's attracted to the complex, multi-faceted agent. But Kade holds secrets he knows Brooke will never understand or accept.

Can Kade keep Brooke safe while coming to terms with his past, or will he stay silent, ruining any future with the woman his heart can't let go?

Always Love You– Book Five
MacLarens of Fire Mountain Contemporary Romance Series
"Romance, adventure, motorcycles, cowboys, suspense—everything you want in a contemporary western romance novel."
Eric Sinclair loves his bachelor status. His work at MacLaren Enterprises leaves him with plenty of time to ride his horse as well as his Harley...and date beautiful women without a thought to commitment.

Amber Anderson is the new person at MacLaren Enterprises. Her passion for marketing landed her what she believes to be the perfect job—until she steps into her first meeting to find the man she left, but still loves, sitting at the management table—his disdain for her clear.

Eric won't allow the past to taint his professional behavior, nor will he repeat his mistakes with Amber, even though love for her pulses through him as strong as ever.

As they strive to mold a working relationship, unexpected danger confronts those close to them, pitting the MacLarens and Sinclairs against an evil who stalks one member but threatens them all.

Eric can't get the memories of their passionate past out of his mind, while Amber wrestles with feelings she thought long buried. Will they be able to put the past behind them to reclaim the love lost years before?

Hearts Don't Lie– Book Six
MacLarens of Fire Mountain Contemporary Romance Series

Mitch MacLaren has reasons for avoiding relationships, and in his opinion, they're pretty darn good. As the new president of RTC Bucking Bulls, difficult challenges occur daily. He certainly doesn't need another one in the form of a fiery, blue-eyed, redhead.

Dana Ballard's new job forces her to work with the one MacLaren who can't seem to get over himself and lighten up. Their verbal sparring is second nature and entertaining until the night of Mitch's departure when he surprises her with a dare she doesn't refuse.

With his assignment in Fire Mountain over, Mitch is free to return to Montana and run the business his father helped start. The glitch in his enthusiasm has to do with one irreversible mistake—the dare Dana didn't ignore. Now, for reasons that confound him, he just can't let it go.

Working together is a circumstance neither wants, but both must accept. As their attraction grows, so do the accidents and strange illnesses of the animals RTC depends on to stay in business. Mitch's total focus should be on finding the reasons and people behind the incidents. Instead, he finds himself torn between his unwanted desire for Dana and the business which is his life.

In his mind, a simple proposition can solve one problem. Will Dana make the smart move and walk away? Or take the gamble and expose her heart?

No Getting Over You– Book Seven
MacLarens of Fire Mountain Contemporary Romance Series

Cassie MacLaren has come a long way since being dumped by her long-time boyfriend, a man she believed to be her future. Successful in her job at MacLaren Enterprises, dreaming of one day leading one of the divisions, she's moved on to start a new relationship, having little time to dwell on past mistakes.

Matt Garner loves his job as rodeo representative for Double Ace Bucking Stock. Busy days and constant travel leave no time for anything more than the occasional short-term relationship—which is just the way he likes it. He's come to accept the regret of leaving the woman he loved for the pro rodeo circuit.
The future is set for both, until a chance meeting ignites long buried emotions neither is willing to face.

Forced to work together, their attraction grows, even as multiple arson fires threaten Cassie's new home of Cold Creek, Colorado. Although Cassie believes the danger from the fires is remote, she knows the danger Matt poses to her heart is real.

While fighting his renewed feelings for Cassie, Matt focuses on a new and unexpected opportunity offered by MacLaren Enterprises—an opportunity that will put him on a direct collision course with Cassie.

Will pride and self-preservation control their future? Or will one be strong enough to make the first move, risking everything, including their heart?

Redemption's Edge – Book One
Redemption Mountain – Historical Western Romance Series

"A heartwarming, passionate story of loss, forgiveness, and redemption set in the untamed frontier during the tumultuous years following the Civil War. Ms. Davies' engaging and complex characters draw you in from the start, creating an exciting introduction to this new historical western romance series."

"Redemption's Edge is a strong and engaging introduction to her new historical western romance series."

Dax Pelletier is ready for a new life, far away from the one he left behind in Savannah following the South's devastating defeat in the Civil War. The ex-Confederate general wants nothing more to do with commanding men and confronting the tough truths of leadership.

Rachel Davenport possesses skills unlike those of her Boston socialite peers—skills honed as a nurse in field hospitals during the Civil War. Eschewing her northeastern suitors and changed by the carnage she's seen, Rachel decides to accept her uncle's invitation to assist him at his clinic in the dangerous and wild frontier of Montana.

Now a Texas Ranger, a promise to a friend takes Dax and his brother, Luke, to the untamed territory of Montana. He'll fulfill his oath and return to Austin, at least that's what he believes.

The small town of Splendor is what Rachel needs after life in a large city. In a few short months, she's grown to love the people as well as the majestic beauty of the untamed frontier. She's settled into a life unlike any she has ever thought possible.

Thinking his battle days are over, he now faces dangers of a different kind—one by those from his past who seek vengeance, and another from Rachel, the woman who's captured his heart.

Wildfire Creek – Book Two
Redemption Mountain – Historical Western Romance Series

"A passionate story of rebuilding lives, working to find a place in the wild frontier, and building new lives in the years following the American Civil War. A rugged, heartwarming story of choices and love in the continuing saga of Redemption Mountain."

Luke Pelletier is settling into his new life as a rancher and occasional Pinkerton Agent, leaving his past as an ex-Confederate major and Texas Ranger far behind. He wants nothing more than to work the ranch, charm the ladies, and live a life of carefree bachelorhood.

Ginny Sorensen has accepted her responsibility as the sole provider for herself and her younger sister. The desire to continue their journey to Oregon is crushed when the need for food and shelter keeps them in the growing frontier town of Splendor, Montana, forcing Ginny to accept work as a server in the local saloon.

Luke has never met a woman as lovely and unspoiled as Ginny. He longs to know her, yet fears his wild ways and unsettled nature aren't what she deserves. She's a girl you marry, but that is nowhere in Luke's plans.

Complicating their tenuous friendship, a twist in circumstances forces Ginny closer to the man she most wants to avoid—the man who can destroy her dreams, and who's captured her heart.

Believing his bachelor status firm, Luke moves from danger to adventure, never dreaming each step he takes brings him closer to his true destiny and a life much different from what he imagines.

Sunrise Ridge – Book Three

Redemption Mountain – Historical Western Romance Series

"The author has a talent for bringing the historical west to life, realistically and vividly, and doesn't shy away from some of the harder aspects of frontier life, even though it's fiction. Recommended to readers who like sweeping western historical romances that are grounded with memorable, likeable characters and a strong sense of place."

Noah Brandt is a successful blacksmith and businessman in Splendor, Montana, with few ties to his past as an ex-Union Army major and sharpshooter. Quiet and hardworking, his biggest challenge is controlling his strong desire for a woman he believes is beyond his reach.

Abigail Tolbert is tired of being under her father's thumb while at the same time, being pushed away by the one man she desires. Determined to build a new life outside the control of her wealthy father, she finds work and sets out to shape a life on her own terms.

Noah has made too many mistakes with Abby to have any hope of getting her back. Even with the changes in her life, including the distance she's built with her father, he can't keep himself from believing he'll never be good enough to claim her.

Unexpected dangers, including a twist of fate for Abby, change both their lives, making the tentative steps they've taken to build a relationship a distant hope. As Noah battles his past as well as the threats to Abby, she fights for a future with the only man she will ever love.

Dixie Moon – Book Four
Redemption Mountain – Historical Western Romance Series

Gabe Evans is a man of his word with strong convictions and steadfast loyalty. As the sheriff of Splendor, Montana, the ex-Union Colonel and oldest of four boys from an affluent family, Gabe understands the meaning of responsibility. The last thing he wants is another commitment—especially of the female variety.
Until he meets Lena Campanel...
Lena's past is one she intends to keep buried.
Overcoming a childhood of setbacks and obstacles, she and her friend, Nick, have succeeded in creating a life of financial success and devout loyalty to one another.
When an unexpected death leaves Gabe the sole heir of a considerable estate, partnering with Nick and Lena is a lucrative decision...forcing Gabe and Lena to work together. As their desire grows, Lena refuses to let down her guard, vowing to keep her past hidden—even from a perfect man like Gabe.
But secrets never stay buried...

When revealed, Gabe realizes Lena's secrets are deeper than he ever imagined. For a man of his character, deception and lies of omission aren't negotiable. Will he be able to forgive the deceit? Or is the damage too great to ever repair?

Survivor Pass – Book Five
Redemption Mountain – Historical Western Romance Series

He thought he'd found a quiet life...
Cash Coulter settled into a life far removed from his days of fighting for the South and crossing the country as a bounty hunter. Now a deputy sheriff, Cash wants nothing more than to buy some land, raise cattle, and build a simple life in the frontier town of Splendor, Montana. But his whole world shifts when his gaze lands on the most captivating woman he's ever seen. And the feeling appears to be mutual.

But nothing is as it seems...
Alison McGrath moved from her home in Kentucky to the rugged mountains of Montana for one reason—to find the man responsible for murdering her brother. Despite using a false identity to avoid any tie to her brother's name, the citizens of Splendor have no intention of sharing their knowledge about the bank robbery which killed her only sibling. Alison knows her circle of lies can't end well, and her growing for Cash threatens to weaken the revenge which drives her.

And the troubles are mounting...
There is danger surrounding them both—men who seek vengeance as a way to silence the past...by any means necessary.

Reclaiming Love – Book One, A Novella

Peregrine Bay – Contemporary Romance Series
Adam Monroe has seen his share of setbacks. Now he's back in Peregrine Bay, looking for a new life and second chance.
Julia Kerrigan's life rebounded after the sudden betrayal of the one man she ever loved. As president of a success real estate company, she's built a new life and future, pushing the painful past behind her.
Adam's reason for accepting the job as the town's new Police Chief can be explained in one word—Julia. He wants her back and will do whatever is necessary to achieve his goal, even knowing his biggest hurdle is the woman he still loves.
As they begin to reconnect, a terrible scandal breaks loose with Julia and Adam at the center.
Will the threat to their lives and reputations destroy their fledgling romance? Can Adam identify and eliminate the danger to Julia before he's had a chance to reclaim her love?

Our Kind of Love – Book Two

Peregrine Bay – Contemporary Romance Series
Selena Kerrigan is content with a life filled with work and family, never feeling the need to take a chance on a relationship—until she steps into a social world inhabited by a man with dark hair and penetrating blue eyes. Eyes that are fixed on her.

Lincoln Caldwell is a man satisfied with his life. Transitioning from an enviable career as a Navy SEAL to becoming a successful entrepreneur, his days focus on growing his security firm, spending his nights with whomever he chooses. Committing to one woman isn't on the horizon—until a captivating woman with caramel eyes sends his personal life into a tailspin.

Believing her identity remains a secret, Selena returns to work, ready to forget about running away from the bed she never should have gone near. She's prepared to put the colossal error, as well as the man she'll never see again, behind her.

Too bad the object of her lapse in judgment doesn't feel the same.

Linc is good at tracking his targets, and Selena is now at the top of his list. It's amazing how a pair of sandals and only a first name can say so much.

As he pursues the woman he can't rid from his mind, a series of cyber-attacks hit his business, threatening its hard-won success. Worse, and unbeknownst to most, Linc harbors a secret—one with the potential to alter his life, along with those he's close to, in ways he could never imagine.
Our Kind of Love, Book Two in the Peregrine Bay Contemporary Romance series, is a full-length novel with an HEA and no cliffhanger.

Colin's Quest – Book One
MacLarens of Boundary Mountain – Historical Western Romance Series

For An Undying Love...
When Colin MacLaren headed west on a wagon train, he hoped to find adventure and perhaps a little danger in

untamed California. He never expected to meet the girl he would love forever. He also never expected her to be the daughter of his family's age-old enemy, but Sarah was a MacGregor and the anger he anticipated soon became a reality. Her father would not be swayed, vehemently refusing to allow marriage to a MacLaren.

Time Has No Effect...
Forced apart for five years, Sarah never forgot Colin—nor did she give up on his promise to come for her. Carrying the brooch he gave her as proof of their secret betrothal, she scans the trail from California, waiting for Colin to claim her. Unfortunately, her father has other plans.

And Enemies Hold No Power.
Nothing can stop Colin from locating Sarah. Not outlaws, runaways, or miles of difficult trails. However, reuniting is only the beginning. Together they must find the courage to fight the men who would keep them apart—and conquer the challenge of uniting two independent hearts.

Find all of my books at:
http://www.shirleendavies.com/books.html

www.ingramcontent.com/pod-product-compliance
Lightning Source LLC
Chambersburg PA
CBHW070956190726
48292CB00004B/1481